The Goodbye Quilt

SUSAN WIGGS

The Goodbye Quilt

MIRA®

MIRA

ISBN-13: 978-0-7783-1322-9

THE GOODBYE QUILT

www.Harlequin.com

Printed in U.S.A.

First Printing: April 2011
10 9 8 7 6 5 4 3 2 1

To my curly-headed daughter, Elizabeth—
you are my sunshine.

DAY ONE

Odometer Reading 121,047

**Wanted: a needle swift enough
to sew this poem into a blanket.**

—Charles Simic,
Serbian-American poet (1938-)

Chapter One

How do you say goodbye to a piece of your heart? If you're a quilter, you have a time-honored way to express yourself.

A quilt is an object of peculiar intimacy. By virtue of the way it is created, every inch of the fabric is touched. Each scrap absorbs the quilter's scent and the invisible oils of her skin, the smell of her household and, thanks to the constant pinning and stitching, her blood in the tiniest of quantities. And tears, though she might be loath to admit it.

My adult life has been a patchwork of projects, most of which were fleeting fancies of overreaching vision. I tend to seize on things, only to abandon them due to a lack of time, talent or inclination. There are a few things I'm truly good at—*Jeopardy!*, riding a bike, balancing a checkbook, orienteering, making balloon animals...and quilting.

I'm good at pulling together little bits and pieces of disparate objects. The process suits me. Each square captures my attention like a new landscape. Everything about quilting suits me, an occupation for hands and heart and imagination.

Other things didn't work out so well—Szechuan cooking, topiary gardening, video games and philately come to mind.

My main project, my ultimate work-in-progress, is Molly, of course. And today she's going away to college, clear across the country. Correction—I'm taking her away, delivering her like an insured parcel to a new life.

Hence the quilt. What better memento to give my daughter than a handmade quilt to keep in her dorm room, a comforter stitched with all the memories of her childhood? It'll be a tangible reminder of who she is, where she comes from...and maybe, if I'm lucky, it will offer a glimpse of her dreams.

All my quilting supplies come from a shop in town called Pins & Needles. The place occupies a vintage building on the main street. It's been in continuous operation for more than five decades. As a child, I passed its redbrick and figured concrete storefront on my way to school each day, and I still remember the kaleidoscope of fabrics in the window, flyers announcing classes and raffles, the rainbow array of rich-colored thread, the treasure trove of glittering notions. My first job as a teenager was at the shop, cutting fabric and ringing up purchases.

When Molly started school, I worked there part time, as much for the extra money as for the company of women who frequented Pins & Needles. Fall is wonderful at the fabric shop, a nesting time, when people are making Halloween costumes, Thanksgiving centerpieces and Christmas decorations. People are never in a hurry in a fabric shop.

They browse. They talk about their projects, giving you a glimpse of their lives.

The shop is a natural gathering place for women. The people I've met there through the years have become my friends. Customers and staff members stand around the cutting tables to discuss projects, give demonstrations and workshops, offer advice on everything from quilting techniques to child rearing to marriage. The ladies there all know about my idea to make a quilt as a going-away gift for Molly. Some of them even created pieces for me to add, embroidered with messages of "Good Luck" and "Congratulations."

You can always tell what's going on in a woman's life based on the quilt she's working on. The new-baby quilts are always light and soft, the wedding quilts pure and clean, filled with tradition, as though a beautiful design might be an inoculation against future strife. Housewarming quilts tend to be artistic, suitable for hanging on an undecorated wall. The most lovingly created quilts of all are the memory quilts, often created as a group project to commemorate a significant event, help with healing or to celebrate a life.

I've always thought a quilt held together with a woman's tears to be the strongest of all.

Nonquilters have a hard time getting their heads around the time and trouble of a project like this. My friend Cherisse, who has three kids, said, "Linda, honey, I'm just glad to get them out of the house—up and running, with no criminal record." Another friend confessed, "My daughter would only ruin it. She's so careless with her things." My neighbor Erin, who started law school when her son entered first grade, now works long hours and makes a ton of money. "I wish I had the time," she said wistfully when I showed her my project.

What I've found is that you make time for the things that matter to you. Everyone *has* the time. It's just a question of deciding what to do with that time. For some people, it's providing for their family. For others, it's finding that precarious balance between taking care of business and the soul-work of being there for husband, children, friends and neighbors.

I'm supposed to be making the last-minute preparations before our departure on the epic road trip, but instead I find myself dithering over the quilt, contemplating sashing and borders and whether my color palette is strong and balanced. Although the top is pieced, the backing and batting in place, there is still much work to be done. Embellishments to add. It might not be proper quilting technique, but quilting is an art, not a science. My crafter's bag is filled with snippets of fabric culled from old, familiar clothes, fabric toys and textiles that have been outgrown, but were too dear or too damaged to take to the Goodwill bin. I'm a big believer in charity bins. Just because a garment is no longer suitable doesn't mean it couldn't be right for someone else. On the other hand, some things are not meant to be parted with.

I sift through the myriad moments of Molly's childhood, which I keep close to my heart, like flowers from a prized bouquet, carefully pressed between sheets of blotter paper. I fold the quilt and put it in the bag with all the bright bits and mementos—a tiny swatch of a babydoll's nightie, an official-looking Girl Scout badge, a precious button that is the only survivor of her first Christmas dress.... So many memories lie mute within this long-handled bag, waiting for me to use them as the final embellishments on this work of art.

I'll never finish in time.

You can do this. I try to give myself a pep talk, but the words fall through my mind and trickle away. This is unexpected, this inability to focus. A panic I haven't been expecting rises up in me, grabbing invisibly at my chest. Breathe, I tell myself. Breathe.

The house already feels different; a heaviness hangs in the drapes over the old chintz sofa. Sounds echo on the wooden floors—a suitcase being rolled to the front porch, a set of keys dropped on the hall table. An air of change hovers over everything.

Dan has driven to the Chevron station to fill the Suburban's tank. He's not coming; this long drive without him will be a first for our family. Until now, every road trip has involved all three of us—Yellowstone, Bryce Canyon, Big Sur, speeding along endless highways with the music turned up loud. We did everything as a family. I can't even remember what Dan and I used to do before Molly. Those days seem like a life that happened to someone else. We were a couple, but Molly made us a family.

This time, Dan will stay home with Hoover, who is getting on in years and doesn't do well at the kennel anymore.

It's better this way. Dan was never fond of saying goodbye. Not that anybody enjoys it, but in our family, I'm always the stoic, the one who makes the emotional work look easy—on the outside, anyway. My solo drive back home will be another first for me. I hope I'll use the time well, getting to know myself again, maybe. Scary thought—what if I get to know myself and I'm someone I don't want to be?

Now, as the heaviness of the impending departure presses down on me, I wonder if we should have planned things differently. Perhaps the three of us should have made this journey together, treating it as a family vacation, like a trip to Disney World or the Grand Canyon.

On the other hand, that's a bad idea. There can be no fooling ourselves into thinking this is something other than what it is—the willful ejection of Molly from our nest. It's too late for second thoughts, anyway. She has to be moved into her dorm in time for freshman orientation. It's been marked on the kitchen calendar for weeks—the expiration date on her childhood.

At the other end of the downstairs, a chord sounds on the piano. Molly tends to sit down and play when she has a lot on her mind. Maybe it's her way of sorting things out.

I'm grateful for the years of lessons she took, even when we could barely afford them. I wanted my daughter to have things I never had, and music lessons are one of them. She's turned into an expressive musician, transforming standard pieces into something heartfelt and mystical. Showy trills and glissandos sluice through the air, filling every empty space in the house. The piano will sit fallow and silent when she's away; neither Dan nor I play. He never had the time to learn; I never had the wherewithal or—I admit it—the patience. Ah, but Molly. She was fascinated with the instrument from the time she stretched up on toddler legs to reach the keys of the secondhand piano we bought at auction. She started lessons when she was only six.

All the hours of practice made up the sound track of her

growing years. "Bill Grogan's Goat" was an early favorite, leading to more challenging works, from "The Rainbow Connection" to "Für Elise," Bartok and beyond. Almost every evening for the past twelve years, Molly practiced while Dan and I cleaned up after dinner. This was her way of avoiding dishwashing duty, and we considered it a fair division of labor—I rinse, he loads, she serenades. She managed to make it to age eighteen without learning to properly load a dishwasher, yet she can play Rachmaninoff.

In the middle of a dramatic pause between chords, a car horn sounds.

The bag with the quilt falls, momentarily forgotten, to the floor. That innocent *yip* of the horn signals that summer has ended.

Molly stops playing, leaving a profound hollow of silence in the house. Seconds later, I can still feel the throb of the notes in the stillness. I go to the landing at the turn of the stairs in time to see her jump up, leaving the piano bench askew.

She runs outside, the screen door snapping shut behind her like a mousetrap. Watching through the window on the landing, I brace myself for another storm of emotion. She has been saying goodbye to Travis all summer long. Today, the farewell will be final.

Here is a picture of Molly: Curly hair wadded into a messy ponytail. Athletic shorts balanced on her hip bones, a T-shirt with a dead rock star on it. A body toned by youth, volleyball and weekend swims at the lake. A face that shows every emotion, even when she doesn't want it to.

Now she flings herself into her boyfriend's arms as a sob breaks from her, mingling with the sound of morning birdsong. Oh, that yearning, the piercing kind only love-dazed teenagers can feel. Hands holding for the last time. Grief written in their posture as their bodies melt together. Travis's arms encircle her with their ropy strength, and his long form bows protectively, walling her off from me.

This kid is both the best and worst kind of boyfriend a mother wants for her daughter. The best, because he's a safe driver and he respects her. The worst, because he incites a passion and loyalty in Molly that impairs her vision of the future.

Last spring, he won her heart like a carnival prize in a ring toss, and they've been inseparable ever since. He is impossibly, irresistibly good-looking, and there's no denying that he's been good to her. He makes no secret of the fact that he doesn't want her to go away. He wants her to feel as if *he* is her next step, not college.

All summer I've been trying to tell her that the right guy wouldn't stand in the way of her dreams. The right guy is going to look at her the way Dan once looked at me, as if he could see the whole world in my face. When Travis regards Molly, he's seeing... not the whole world. His next weekend, maybe.

Hoover lifts his leg and pees on the tire of Travis's Camaro, the guy's pride and joy. Travis and Molly don't notice.

I can't hear their conversation, but I can see his mouth shape the words: *Don't go.*

My heart echoes the sentiment. I want her to stay close, too. The difference is, I know she needs to leave.

Molly speaks; I hope she's telling him she has to go away, that this opportunity is too big to miss. She has won a scholarship to a world-class private university. She's getting a chance at a life most people in our small western Wyoming town never dream of. Here in a part of the state that appears roadless and sparse on travel maps, life moves slowly. Our town is filled with good people, harsh weather and a sense that big dreams seem to come true only when you leave. The main industry here is a plant that makes prefab log homes.

I turn away from the window, giving Molly her private farewell. She is far more upset about leaving Travis than about leaving Dan and me, a fact that is hard to swallow.

Dan comes back from the service station. He visits with Travis briefly. I compare the two of them as they stand together talking. Dan is solidly built, his shoulders and arms sculpted by his years at the plant before he made supervisor. He looks as grounded and dependable as the pickup truck he drives. By contrast, Travis is tall and lithe with youth, his slender body curving into a question mark as he gestures with pride at his cherry-red car.

The two of them shake hands; then Dan heads inside. Our eyes meet and skate away; we're not ready to talk yet. In the kitchen, the two of us make a few final preparations—bundling road maps together, adding ice to the cooler of drinks.

Summer glares against the screen door, its hot scent a reminder that the day is already a few hours old. I think of a thousand other summer days, whiled away without a care for the slow passing of time. We built a tree house, went on bike rides, hung a rope swing over a swimming hole, made sno-cones, watched ants on the march. We lay faceup in the grass and stared at clouds until our eyes watered. We fought about curfews, shopped for back-to-school supplies, sang along with songs on the radio. We laughed at nothing until our sides ached, and cried at movies with sad endings.

I sneak a glance at Dan. I can't picture him crying at the movies with me. That was always Molly's role, the exclusive domain of females. Without really planning to, she and I created rituals and traditions, and these things formed a powerful bond.

There is a vehemence to the thoughts tearing through my head, a sense of rebellion—How can I just let her go? I didn't sign up for this—for creating my greatest work only to have to shove her away from me.

When I pushed her out into the world, she was handed immediately into my arms. I never thought of letting her go, only of holding her next to my heart, under which she'd grown, already adored by the time she made her appearance. The idea of her leaving was an abstraction, a nonspecified Someday. Now it's all happening, exactly as we planned. Except I didn't plan for it to throttle me.

Dan seems easy about the process. He's always accepted—even welcomed—life's movements from one phase to the next, like birthdays or promotions at work. He is the sort of person who makes life look effortless, a trait I admire and sometimes envy in him.

As for me, I find myself unable to move. I'm not ready. This wrenching grief has blindsided me. I didn't expect it to be this intense. All kids leave home. That's the way it works. If you do your job of parenting correctly, this is the end result. They leave. When it *doesn't* work that way, that's when a mother should worry. If the kid sticks around, takes up permanent residence in her childhood bedroom, you're considered a failure.

Ah, but the price of succeeding is a piece of your soul. I bite my lip to keep from trying to explain this to Dan. He would tell me I'm being overly dramatic. Maybe so, but everything about this process *feels* dramatic. This child has been the focus of every day of my life for the past eighteen years. After being a parent for so long, I am forced to surrender the role. Now, all of a sudden, a void has opened up.

Snap out of it, I tell myself. I have so much to be thankful for—this rich, full life. Health, husband and home. And lots to look forward to. It's wrong to mope and wallow in the tragedy of it all. What's the matter with me?

The matter is this—I'm facing a huge loss. The biggest part of my daughter's life is about to start, and it doesn't include me and Dan. Granted, we've had plenty of time to prepare, but now that the moment has arrived, it's as unexpectedly painful as a sudden accident.

Although greeting card companies have created themes around every possible life event, there's no ritual for this particular transition.

This is surprising, because when a child leaves for college, it is the end of something. Other than birth or death, leaving home for any reason is the most extreme of life transitions. One moment we're a family of three. The next, we've lost a vital member. It's a true loss, only people don't understand your grief. They don't send you sympathy cards or invite you to join a support group. They don't flock to comfort you. They don't come to your door bearing tuna casseroles and bottles of Cold Duck and platters of cookies on their good chintz china.

Instead, the journey to college is a rite of passage we mark as a joyous occasion, one we celebrate by buying luggage and books on how to build a fulfilling life. But really, if you ask any mother, she'll tell you that deep down, we want to mark it as a loss, a funeral of sorts. We never show our sorrow, though. Our sadness stays in the shadows like something slightly shameful.

Travis leaves, peeling himself away like a Band-aid that's been stuck on too long. His union job at the plant keeps him on a strict schedule; he cannot linger. Molly stands on the front sidewalk and watches his Camaro growing smaller and smaller down the tree-lined street, flanked by timber frame houses from the 1920s, remnants of the days when this was a company town. Molly's face is stiff and pale, as if she's been shocked and disoriented by unexpected pain. Her arms are folded across her middle.

I hurry outside, wanting to comfort her. "I know it's hard," I say, giving her a hug.

She is stiff and unyielding, regarding me like an intruder. "You have no idea how this feels," she says. "You never had to leave Dad."

She's right. Dan and I met at a bar twenty-some years ago, and after our first dance together, we already knew we'd be a couple. If somebody had told me I had to leave him and head off to a world of strangers, would I have been willing to do that? Yes, shouts a seldom-heard voice inside me—oh, yes.

Molly waits for an answer.

"Aw, Moll. Your dad and I were in a much different place—"

"Nobody forced you two apart," she says, her voice rising.

"And nobody's forcing you and Travis apart."

"Then why am I leaving? Why am I going thousands of miles away?"

"Because it's what you've always wanted, Molly."

"Maybe I've changed my mind. Maybe I should stay and go to college in state."

"We need to finish loading the car," I tell her.

We argue. Loudly, in the driveway. About what won't fit in the car. About what is necessary, what Molly will not be able to do without. She flounces into the house and returns a few minutes later with a duffel bag and a green-shaded lamp.

"Sweetie, I don't think you need the lamp," I point out.

"I want to bring it. I've always liked this lamp." She crams the duffel bag in the back, using it to cushion the lamp.

It has shone over her desk while she worked diligently at connect-the-dots, a report on Edward Lear, a tear-stained journal, a labored-over college essay, a love letter to Travis Spellman. The lamp has been a silent sentinel through the years. Remembering this, I quickly surrender. I don't want to argue anymore, especially not today.

Like making the quilt, driving her to college seemed like a good idea at the time. She could have flown, and shipped her things separately, but I couldn't stand the thought of leaving her at the curb at the airport like a houseguest who's overstayed her welcome.

A road trip just seemed so appealing, a final adventure for the two of us to share. A farewell tour. All through the summer I've been picturing us in the old Suburban, stuffed to the top with things Molly will need in the freshman dorm, singing along with the radio and reminiscing about old times. Now as I face the sullen rebellion in Molly's face, the idyllic picture dissipates.

The trip is still a good idea, though. A long drive with no one but each other for company will give us a chance to talk about matters we've been avoiding all summer long, possibly her entire adolescence. When she was little, we discussed the great matters of her life at bedtime, lying together in the dark, watching the play of moon shadows on the ceiling. In high school, she stayed up later than I did, and our conversations shrank to sleepy utterances. Nighttime was punctuated by the creak of a floorboard under a furtive foot, the rasp of a toothbrush washing away the smell of a sneaked beer. Some days, we barely spoke a half-dozen words.

I want these long, empty hours with her on the road. I need them with an intensity that I hide from Molly, because I don't want her to worry that I'm getting desperate. She's a worrier, my Molly. A pleaser. She wants everyone to be happy, and if she had some inkling of how I'm feeling right now, she'd try to do something about it. I don't want her to feel as if she's responsible for my happiness. Good lord, who would wish that on a child?

We finish packing. Everything is in order, every checklist completed, our iPods organized with music and podcasts, every contact duly entered in our mobile phones. Finally, the moment has arrived.

"Well," says Dan. "I guess that's it."

What's it? I wonder. What? But I smile and say, "Yep. Ready, kiddo?"

"In a minute," she says, stooping and patting her leg to call the dog.

I am unprepared for the wrench as she says goodbye to Hoover. We adopted the sweet-faced Lab mix as a pup when Molly was four. They grew up together—littermates, we used to call them, laughing at their rough-and-tumble antics. Since then, she has shared every important moment with the dog—holidays, neighborhood walks and summer campouts, fights with friends, Saturday morning cartoons, endless tosses of slimy tennis balls.

Through the years, Hoover has endured wearing doll clothes and sunglasses, being pushed in a stroller, taken to school for show-and-tell, and sneaked under the covers on cold winter nights. These days, he has slowed down, and is now as benign and endearing as a well-loved velveteen toy. None of us dares to acknowledge what we all know—that he will be gone by the time Molly finishes college.

She hunkers down in front of him, cradling his muzzle between her hands in the way I've seen her do ten thousand times before. She burrows her face into his neck and whispers something. Hoover gives a soft groan of contentment, loving the attention. When she draws away, he tries to reel her back in with a lifted front paw—*Shake, boy*. Molly rises slowly, grasps the paw for a moment, then gently sets it down.

Next, she turns to Dan. I notice the stiff set of his shoulders and the way he checks and rechecks everything—tires, cell phone batteries, wiper fluid. I can see him checking Molly, too, but she doesn't recognize the pain in his probing looks. He hides behind a mask of bravado, reassuring to his daughter but transparent to me.

Their goodbye mirrors their history together through the years—loving, a little awkward. He's never been one to show his emotions, but he was the one who taught her to swim, to laugh, to belch on command, to throw a baseball overhand, to pump up a bicycle tire, to eat smoked oysters straight out of the can, to flatten pennies on railroad tracks.

Their farewell is perfunctory, almost casual. They both seem to possess a quiet understanding that their lives are meant to intersect and diverge. "Call me tonight," he says. "Call me whenever you want."

"Sure, Dad. Love you."

They hug. He kisses her on the crown of her head. His hand lingers on her arm; she doesn't meet his eyes. Sunlight glances off the car window as she gets in.

Dan comes around to the other side and kisses me, his lips warm and familiar. "Take care, Linda," he says in a husky voice, the same thing he always says to me, but today the words carry extra weight.

"Of course," I say, holding him for an extra beat. Then I whisper in his ear, "How will I get through this?"

He pulls back, giving me a quizzical look. "Because you will," he says simply. "You can do anything, Lindy."

I smile to acknowledge the kind words, but I'm not certain I trust them.

The rearview mirror frames a view of our boxy, painted house, where we've lived since before Molly was born. Not for the first time, it hits me that I'll come home to an empty nest. People say this stage of life is a golden time, filled with possibility. Someone—probably a woman with too many kids and pets—once said the true definition of freedom is when the last child leaves home and the dog dies. At last, you get your life back. Your time is your own. The trouble is—and I can't bear to admit this, even to Dan—I never said I wanted it back.

As we pull out onto the street, he stands and watches us go, the dog leaning against his leg. My husband braces an arm on the front gate and lowers his head. When I get back from this journey, he and I will be alone again, the way we were eighteen years ago, before the explosion of love that was Molly, before late-night feedings and bouts of the croup, before scary movies and argued-over curfews, before pranks and laughter, tempests and tears.

With Molly gone, we'll have all this extra space in our lives. I'll have to look him in the eye and ask, "Are you still the same person I married?" Or maybe the real question is, *Am I?*

I picture us seated across the dinner table from each other, night after night. What will we talk about? Do we know everything about each other, or is there still more to discover? I can't recall the last time I asked him about his dreams and desires, or the last time he asked me something more than "Did you feed the dog this morning?"

I invested so much more time in Molly over the years. When there's a daughter keeping us preoccupied, it's easy to slip away from each other.

With all my heart, I hope it's equally easy to reach across the divide. I suppose I'll find out soon enough.

Chapter Two

I don't even bother offering to drive. Molly insists on driving everywhere, and has done so ever since she turned sixteen. At the moment this is a convenient arrangement. I can use the time to work on the quilt. I'm picturing the completed piece at the other end of the journey—warm and soft, a tangible reminder of Molly's past. Each bit of fabric is a puzzle piece of her childhood, tessellating with the others around it. All that remains is to finish quilting the layers together, adding more embellishments along the way.

Working by hand rather than machine is soothing, and the pattern is free-form within the wooden hoop. On the solid pieces of fabric, words and messages can be embedded like secrets in code: *Courage. You're beautiful. Walk it off. Freud was wrong.* I should declare the thing finished by now but, like a nesting magpie, I keep adding bright trinkets—a button from a favorite sweater, a blue ribbon from a piano recital, a vintage handkerchief and a paste earring that belonged to her grandmother. There's some old, faded fabric from Molly's kindergarten apron, green with little laughing monkey heads. And a bow from her prom corsage, worn with shining pride just a few months ago.

Though it's impossible to be objective, I know this thing I have created is beautiful, even with all its flaws. Even though it's not finished. This is a record of her days with me, from the moment I realized I was pregnant—I was working in the garden, wearing a yellow dotted halter top, which is now part of the quilt—to today. Yes, even today I grabbed Hoover's favorite bandanna to incorporate.

Like so many projects I've tackled over the years—like parenting itself—the quilt is ambitious and unwieldy. But maybe the hours of enforced idleness in the car will be just what I need to add the final flourishes.

As we drive along the main street of our town, Molly looks out at the flower baskets on the streetlamp poles, the little coffee stands and cafés, the bank and bike shop and bookstore, the fashion boutiques and galleries advertising fall sales, the congregational church with its painted white spire. There's the stationery shop, advertising back-to-school specials, and of course, Pins & Needles, my favorite place in town. The charming old building stands shoulder-to-shoulder between a bakery and a boutique, sharing a concrete keystone that marks the year it was built—1902. Arched windows in the upper stories, which house an optometrist and a chiropractor, are decked with wrought-iron window boxes filled with asters and mums. On the street level is the abundant display window, replete with fabrics in the delicious colors of autumn—pumpkin and amber, flame red, magenta, shadowy purple.

A small, almost apologetic-looking sign in the window says, "Business For Sale." Minerva, the shop owner, is retiring and she's been looking for a buyer since the previous Christmas. She's told all her customers that if it's not sold by the new year, she'll simply close its doors. This option is looking more and more likely. It's hard to imagine someone with the kind of passion and energy it takes—not to mention the capital—to run a small shop. Once the store is cleared to the bare walls, it will look like a blight on our town's main street, a missing tooth in the middle of a smile. On top of Molly going away, it's another blow.

Across the street is a trendy clothing boutique where Molly has spent many an hour—and many a dollar—agonizing over just the right look. As she was trying on jeans the other day, a debate ensued. Do girls on the East Coast wear skinny jeans or boot cut? Do they even wear hoodies? As if I would know these things. When she began worrying about what to wear, I realized that everything was getting very real for Molly. For a girl who has never lived anywhere else, this is a huge step. Now that we're on the road, she is facing the reality that college is an actual place, not just a display of glossy pictures in a catalog. I want to tell her not to be afraid, but I suspect the advice wouldn't be welcome.

Navigating the ungainly Suburban up the ramp to the interstate, Molly fiddles with the radio, but it's all talk so she switches it off. We've got our iPods if we're desperate for music.

From the grim look on Molly's face as she cranes her neck to check the rearview mirror, it's clear that she knows I was right about the lamp taking up too much space. I can't help thinking what I won't allow myself to say: I told you so.

Agitated, I put on my discount-store reading glasses—the ones that perch on my nose and make me look like a schoolmarm. Another visible rite of passage. For me, the moment occurred a few years back, when I turned thirty-nine-and-a-half. I was in a gift shop, trying to read a sale tag, and suddenly my arm wasn't quite long enough to make out the price.

A sales clerk offered me a pair of reading glasses, and the fine print came into focus. The fact that the glasses had cute faux-Burberry frames offered scant comfort. At first, I was a bit embarrassed to put them on around Dan and Molly, but when you love needlework and crossword puzzles as much as I do, you swallow your pride.

I open the canvas quilt bag and the project spills across my lap. The oval hoop frames a section made of a calico maternity blouse I wore while carrying Molly. I stab the needle in, telling myself it'll be finished soon enough, one stitch after another. The needle flashes in and out like a little silver dart.

"Bad intersection up here," I say, glancing up when we reach the crossroads leading to the interstate. "Be sure you signal."

"Hello. I've only been through this intersection a zillion times. And did you know that at eighteen, a person's vision is performing at its peak?"

I adjust my glasses. "So is her smart mouth." My needle starts writing the words "be sweet," adding a curlicue at the end.

"I'm just saying, don't worry about my driving. I learned from the best."

This is true. Dan's an excellent driver, alert and confident, traits he passed along to our daughter. Most of her friends learned through Driver's Ed, but money was tight that year due to a layoff, and Dan did the honors. I used to wonder what they talked about during all those hours of practice, but when I asked, they both offered blank looks. "We didn't talk about anything."

What she means is, Dan has a way of communicating without talk. He can speak volumes with a glance, a chuckle or a shrug. The two of them are comfortable in their silence in the way Molly and I are comfortable nattering away at each other.

Sure enough, there's a small tangle of traffic at the intersection, but I bite my tongue. Literally, I press my teeth into my tongue. I will not speak up. The time is past for correcting my daughter, giving directives. These final days together should be special, sacred almost, the last slender thread of a bond that has endured for eighteen years and is about to be willfully severed.

Molly expertly accelerates up the on-ramp and merges smoothly with the flow of traffic. She keeps her eyes on the road, her profile delicate and clean-lined, startlingly adult.

It's a bright September morning, and the lingering heat of late summer shimmers, turning the asphalt into a river of mercury. With a flick of her little finger, Molly signals and moves into the swift current of the middle lane. She is a competent driver, skilled, even. She's competent and skilled at many things—water polo, trigonometry, getting rid of phone solicitors, being a good friend.

Her spirit, her self-assurance and independence, are the sort of wonderful qualities a mother wants in her daughter. My goal was always to raise a child capable of making judgments on her own. Teaching her has been a joyous process, while actually seeing her go off in her own direction is intensely bittersweet. Adulthood, I suppose, is the final exam to see which lessons she absorbed.

"What do you suppose your father's doing?" I ask, picturing Dan alone in the house. For the next several days, his diet will consist only of things that can be made from tortilla chips, cheese and cold cuts.

Molly shrugs. Her shiny dark curls spring with the motion. "He's probably breaking out the cigars."

I think of him standing on the driveway this morning, giving his daughter an awkward hug before stepping back, stiff-faced, his eyes shining. I wonder if she looked in the rearview mirror as we pulled away, if she saw her father bow his head, then lean down to pet the dog.

"Oh, come on," I chide her. "Is that what you really think?"

"I don't know. I figure he's been looking forward to this day for a long time. Dad's good with change."

Meaning I'm not. And although he might be good with this particular change, there's a part of him that has come unmoored. Dan loves Molly with both a consuming flame and a heart-pounding fear. Their complicated relationship has always been full of contradictions. Dan was in the delivery room when Molly was born on a cold February morning eighteen years ago, and the moment the baby appeared in all her pulsing, slippery, newborn glory, he wept, the tears soaking into the paper surgical mask they'd made him wear. The first time Molly was placed in his arms, he held the tiny bundle with the shocked immobility of abject terror. He hadn't smiled down into the red, wrinkled face, not the way I did, instantly a mother, with a mother's serene confidence and a sense of accomplishment so intense I was floating. He hadn't cooed and swayed to that universal internal lullaby all mothers begin to hear the moment the baby is laid in their arms. He had simply stood and looked as though someone had handed him a vial of nitroglycerin.

Yet last night, I awakened to find him crying. He was absolutely silent, but the bed quivered with his fight to keep from making a sound. I said nothing, but lay perfectly still, helplessly drifting. Have I lost the ability to comfort him? Maybe I just didn't want to intrude. We are each dealing with the departure of our only child in our own way. When you're married, you don't get to be let in, not to everything.

"Trust me," I assure Molly. "He's going to miss you like crazy."

"He never said so."

"He wouldn't. But that doesn't mean he won't be missing you every single second."

"I guess."

Too often, there's a disconnect between Dan and Molly, despite the undeniable fact that they love each other. I pause, frowning at a knot that has formed in my thread. "That's just the way he is," I tell Molly. This is my role—the go-between, translating for the two of them.

I tease the knot loose and go back to my stitching. The border abuts a trapezoid-shaped swatch of neutral-colored lawn, snipped from the dress she wore to the eighth-grade banquet, the first grown-up dance of her life. At age thirteen she was impossible, taking drama to new heights and sullenness to new depths. I used to try to turn our dirgelike family dinners into something a little more upbeat. "What's the highlight of your day?" I used to ask my husband and daughter. "What's the one thing that makes it worth getting up in the morning?"

Dan had been grinding pepper on his salad in that deliberate way of his. Barely looking up, he said, "When Molly smiles at me."

He startled both Molly and me with that remark. And our sullen, teenage daughter had smiled at him.

Now Molly's phone rings with a familiar tone—an Eddie Vedder song called "The Face of Love." It's Travis's ringtone.

A heartbreaking softness suffuses her face as she picks up. "Hi," she says, her voice as intimate as a lover's. "I'm driving." She listens for a moment, then ends with a "Yeah, me, too," and closes the phone.

More silence. The needle darts. The day slides by the car windows. Prairie towns between endless grasslands. We make a pit stop, eat some junk food, talk about nothing. Same as we always do.

Odometer Reading 121,633

"...it may have been some unconsciously craved compensation for the drab monotony of their days that caused the women...to evolve quilt patterns so intricate. Only a soul in desperate need of nervous outlet could have conceived and executed, for instance, the 'Full Blown Tulip...'"

– Ruth E. Finley,
Old Patchwork Quilts and the Women Who Made Them (1929)

Chapter Three

"Remember this one?" I ask, angling part of the quilt into Molly's line of vision.

"I guess."

"I bet you don't remember it."

"Then why did you ask? You always do that, Mom."

"Do I? I never noticed."

"You're always quizzing me about stuff you think should be important to me."

"Really? Yikes." I brush my hand over the piece of purple cotton, covered by lace.

"So what about that one?" She is instantly suspicious. All summer long, little "do-you-remembers" and "last times" have sneaked in—the last time we drove to the lake at the county line to set off fireworks, the last time Dan and I attended one of her piano recitals, the last time she went for a haircut at the Twirl & Curl.

"It's from a dress your father bought you," I say, needle

pushing in and out, running a line of stitches to spell out *Daddy's girl.*

"Dad bought me a dress? No way."

"He did, at the Mexican Marketplace. I can't believe you forgot."

"Mom. What was I, three or four years old?"

"Four, I think."

"I rest my case."

In my mind's eye, I can still see her turning in front of the hall mirror, showing off the absurd confection of purple cotton and cheap lace. "It swirls," Molly had shouted, spinning madly. "It *swirls!*" I was less charmed when she insisted on wearing it to church for the next nine weeks. The dress fell apart years ago, but there was enough fabric left to work into the quilt.

Memories flow past in a swift smear of color, like the warehouses and billboards lining the interstate. When I shut my eyes, I can picture so many moments, frozen in time. So many details, sharp as a captured image—the wisp of my newborn baby's hair, the sweet curve of her cheek as she nurses. I can still imagine the drape of her christening gown, which is wrapped in tissue now, stored in the bottom of the painted cedar chest in the guestroom. I can clearly see myself poking a spoonful of white cereal into a round little birdlike mouth. I see Molly spring forward on chubby legs off the side of the pool, into my outstretched arms.

All those firsts. The first day of kindergarten: Molly wore her hair in two tight pigtails, her plaid jumper ironed in crisp pleats, her backpack filled with waxy-smelling new crayons, sharpened pencils, lined paper, a lunch I'd spent forty-five minutes preparing.

"Do you remember your first day of school?" I ask her now, flourishing the part of the quilt made of the uniform blouse.

"Sure. My teacher was Miss Robinson, and I carried a Mulan lunch box." Molly changes lanes and eases past a poky hybrid car. "You put a note in my lunch. I always liked it when you did that."

I don't recall the teacher or the lunch box, but I definitely remember the note, the first of many I would tuck into Molly's lunch over the years. I always tried to write a few words on a paper napkin with a little smiling cartoon mommy, with squiggles to represent my hair, and the message "I ♥ U. Love, Mommy."

I tried to upgrade my wardrobe for the occasion, wearing slacks, Weejuns and coral lip gloss from a department store counter. I felt important, compelled by mission and duty, as Molly chattered gleefully in the back of my station wagon.

Stopping at the tree-shaded curb of the school, I pretended to be calm and cheerful as I kissed Molly's cheek, stroked her head and then smilingly waved goodbye. She met up with her friends Amber and Rani. The girls went inside together, giggling and skipping the whole way, into the redbrick institution that suddenly looked huge and forbidding to me.

There was a New Mothers' coffee in the library. At the meeting, we moms worked out party plans and carpool arrangements with the sober attention of battle commanders. I felt secretly intimidated—not by the working moms in their power suits and high heels. On some level I understood they were as scared and uncertain as I was, even with their advanced degrees and job titles.

No, I was overawed by the stay-at-home moms. They were the gold standard we all aspired to. They seemed so organized and poised, in khakis with earth-tone sweaters looped negligently over their shoulders, datebooks open in front of them, monogrammed pens poised to make notes. Independent yet obviously supported by the unseen infrastructure of husbands and homeowners' associations, they were eminently comfortable in their own skin.

To this day, I don't remember driving home after handing my child over to a new phase of life. All I remember is bursting into the house, sitting down at the breakfast counter with the view of the jungle gym Dan had built in the backyard, and shaking with a sense of emptiness I hadn't expected to feel. Even Hoover, huddled in confusion at my feet, couldn't cheer me up. But back then, hope had glimmered at the end of the day. Molly would come home, she'd eat pecan sandies and drink a glass of milk while chattering on about kindergarten, and all would be well.

Although years have passed since that bright August morning, I never quite mastered the put-together look or the air of confidence I observed in my peers. I didn't really fit in with the stay-at-homes, but I wasn't a career woman, either. A scattershot woman, you might call me, aiming myself in different directions, my only true calling that of loving my family.

I kept meaning to find something—a vocation, a passion, a marketable way to spend my time. But after Molly was born, the quest simply didn't seem to matter so much. Unconcerned with a career trajectory, I bounced around to a few different jobs, never quite finding the right fit. This didn't bother me, because without really planning it, I had lucked into a life I loved so much I never wanted it to change. The quilt shop became my second home. I loved the creative energy of the shop, the dry smell of the fabric, the crisp metallic bite of my super-sharp scissors on the cutting table. Working at Minerva's shop became more than a part-time job during the school year. It was a place of refuge from the empty hours of the school day.

Molly glances over; I see her watching my busy hands.

"What?" I ask.

"Did you know Athena is the goddess of quilting?"

"She's the Warrior Woman," I correct her. "It's one of the few things I remember from mythology."

"Most people don't know she's also the goddess of arts and crafts," Molly says, full of authority, the way she gets sometimes. "Domestic crafts require planning and strategy, too. That's how the logic goes, anyway."

"Athena was superwoman, then. Waging war and weaving baskets." I settle back with the quilt draped over my lap and try to focus on feeling like a goddess. My stitches meander into overlapping spirals. These will be a reminder of the cyclical nature of families, the comings and goings of generations. They say a child leaves home in phases. She is weaned: Molly weaned herself as soon as she learned to walk, preferring a binky she could carry around in her pocket. Then she starts school. Goes on her first sleepover. To sleep-away camp. A field trip to the state capitol. She learns to drive, and each time she heads out the door, it takes her out of reach, on her own. This is simply the next step in the process. She'll be fine. I'll be fine.

I swear.

"I spotted an *A*," Molly says abruptly, bringing me back

to the present. "The Aladdin Motel. And there's a *B*—Uncle Porky's Burger Barn...."

The hunt is on—an old alphabet game we used to play on long car trips. We quickly find our way through to the letter *J,* calling out names of towns and cafés, cribbed from highway signs, billboards and truck stops. The town of Jasper keeps the game moving. The *Q* is found on a hand-lettered roadside "Bar-B-Q," and we are grateful for colloquial spelling habits. We never get stuck on *X*, thanks to the freeway exit signs, and *Z* is found on a radio station billboard, KIZZ: Downhome Country for Uptown Folks.

In a Big Boy restaurant in Franklin, a young mother is trying to work the newspaper Sudoku puzzle while her toddler, strapped into a little wooden high chair, makes monkeyshines to get her attention. He leans as far sideways as the high chair permits, makes a sound like a cat, bangs his fork on the table, crams dry Cheerios into his mouth and uses a chicken nugget to smear ketchup on his tray like a baby Jackson Pollock. The young mother tucks her hair behind her ear and fills in another blank space on the puzzle.

I want to rush across the dining room and shake the woman. Can't you see he needs you to look at him? Play with him, will you, already? It'll be over before you know it.

It's easy to recognize a little of myself in the weary, distracted young mother. I used to be like her—preoccupied with matters of no importance, never seeing the secretive, invisible passage of time slip by until it was gone. Yet if someone had deigned to point this out, I would have been baffled, maybe even indignant. Disregard my child? What do you take me for?

However, when you're with a toddler who takes forty-five minutes to eat a chicken nugget, the moments drag. Or when your baby has the croup at 3:00 a.m. and you're sitting in the bathroom with the steam on full blast, crying right along with her because you're both so tired and miserable—those nights seem to have no end.

From my perspective at the other end of childhood, I want to tell the young mother what I know now—that when a child is little, the days roll by at a leaden pace, blurring together. You're like a cartoon character, blithely oblivious while crossing a precarious wooden bridge, never knowing it's on fire behind you, burning away as you go. Sure, everybody says to enjoy your kids while they're little, because they'll be grown before you know it, but nobody ever really believes it. The woman at the next table simply wouldn't see the bridge, see time eating up the moments like a fire-breathing dragon.

Fortunately for everyone involved, even I'm not crazy enough to intrude. For all I know, she's got a load of worries on her mind, or maybe she just needs ten minutes to dream her own dreams. Maybe she craves the neat, precise order of a Sudoku puzzle as a reminder that everything has a solution. By the time she finishes her puzzle, the kid has given up on her and finished his Cheerios and nugget. She wipes his face and hands, scoops him up and plants a perfunctory kiss on his head as she goes to the register.

Molly has missed the exchange entirely. She is absorbed in paging through the college's glossy catalog. The booklet depicts an idyllic world where the grass is preternaturally green and weedless, buildings stand the test of time and students are eternally young, sitting around in earnest groups or laughing together over lattes. Professors look appropriately smart, many of them cultivating a kind of bohemian quirkiness that, in our hometown, would probably cause them to fall under suspicion.

"See anything you like?" I ask as she pauses on a page of course descriptions.

"Everything," she states, her eyes dancing. "There's a whole course called 'Special Topics in Women's Suffrage Music.' And 'Transgender Native American Art.' 'The Progressive Pottery Experience: Ideas in Transition.'" She struggles to keep a straight face. "I want it all."

We have a laugh, and I can feel her excitement. The catalog is a treasure trove of possibilities, new things for her to learn, ways to think, ideas about life, maybe even a way to change the world.

Though I'm thrilled for her, I feel a silly twinge of envy. There are matters Dan and I can't begin to teach her, I remind myself. That's what college is for.

"I have no clue how I'm going to pick," she says, her hand smoothing the pages.

"I wouldn't know where to begin." The admission masks an old ambivalence. I had always meant to finish college and even had a plan. For many people, this didn't seem particularly bold, but in my family, it was a big step. Neither of my parents had gone to college; their own parents were immigrants and higher education was simply out of reach for them. My folks regarded college as an unnecessary frill, an expensive four-year procrastination before you get to the real part of life.

My dad worked as a shift supervisor at the tile plant. My mom stayed home with us and ironed. Really, she did. She took in ironing. We saw nothing unusual about this. There was never any shame, no judgment. It was who we were, and we were perfectly happy together. The house often smelled of the dry warmth of a heated iron and spray starch. There was a little rate sheet posted behind the kitchen door. People would leave their stuff in a basket by the milk box on the back stoop in the morning; Mom would iron it and the next day, my big brother Jonas would deliver the items—crisply pressed dress shirts and knife-pleated slacks for the plant executives, party dresses and St. Cecilia's uniform blouses for their wives and kids.

I never really thought about what went through my mom's mind as she stood at the ironing board, perfecting the details of other people's clothing while Dire Straits played on the radio. Now I wonder if she was hot. Uncomfortable. Resigned. Or maybe she liked ironing and the work made her happy.

I wish I'd asked her. I wish she was still around, so I could ask her now.

Instead, eager for my independence, I planned my future. My dreams were nurtured by hours and hours in the library, reading books about women who created amazing lives for themselves, studying music and painting, science and business. I swore one day when I was a mother, I would instill these dreams in my children. I would be the mother I wanted my mother to be. And so I made a plan.

After high school, I would spend the summer working to save up money for tuition. Both my parents shook their heads, unable to fathom the idea of putting off work and life and independence for another four years, at the end of which there would be a massive debt and no guarantee of success. Besides, the closest university was nearly two hours away.

It was a powerful dream—maybe *too* powerful, because to someone raised the way I was, it seemed more like a fantasy. Particularly when I tallied up the cost of living without income for four years. Particularly when reality came crashing down on me, first semester. For monetary reasons, I had to live at home and quickly found the commute in my second-hand Gremlin to be almost unbearable. Later, I shared an apartment near campus with some friends, returning home each weekend with a sack of laundry. Worse, my classes were boring, keeping my grades decent was a struggle and dealing with a couple of bad professors nearly broke me.

Then Dan came along, Dan Davis with his incredible eyes, strong craftsman's hands, his sturdy work ethic and air of assuredness. In his arms, I realized the true meaning of happiness. My dreams of some nebulous *someday* stopped making sense in the face of such overwhelming happiness.

I once read in a book somewhere that the way you spend your day is the way you spend your life. Did I want a life of days filled with rushing back and forth on a commute, juggling coursework and having barely enough time for Dan? Or a life nurturing the love I'd found with him?

A no-brainer. We got married, Dan worked harder than ever so we could buy a house, and I got a job working retail. Don't ask me where. There are too many places to count. I put off returning to college; the plan kept being pushed back by the unending forward march of bills, and the sheer bliss of spending my time loving Dan, making a home, creating our life together.

After Dan and I married, I didn't exactly drop out of school, I just stopped going. There were a hundred rationalizations for this. Tuition was costly, and we wanted to save up for a house. The commute to campus took too much time and gas money. It seemed self-indulgent to spend our hard-earned money on classes like "Special Topics in Esoteric Cubism."

And then one day, after we'd been married a few years, the idea of getting a degree was taken off the table. We did use contraception, I swear we did, but mother nature and youthful zeal overrode the precautions. Along came Molly, the ultimate—and only truly valid—excuse for interrupting my education.

I always meant to go back. Early on, I told my friends and family I planned to finish my degree once Molly was in grade school. Of course, by then I knew what all mothers learn when their kids go to school. Those hours are spoken for, too. They're filled with everything else you put off when your child is young and at home, with that part-time job to give the bank account a much-needed boost. With Brownie projects and volunteer service. With taking care of that little female problem that's had you so worried for so long. With adding on an extra bathroom to the house—she's going to need that once she hits her teens, after all. Throwing in college-level courses simply seems impossible.

Nobody was surprised when I dropped the idea. My parents were simple, honest people who expected their kids to live a good life. I hope I didn't disappoint them.

My departure from the nest was not the dramatic, long-distance leap Molly is taking. My first home with Dan was only eight miles from my parents.

I wonder if they dreamed of a bigger life for me, if they wanted me to go further, do more. Probably not, I think, watching my needle flash through the fabric. I suspect they were perfectly content for their daughter to live close by.

My friend Erin wears her hard-earned law degree like a badge of pride. I used to envy her—the big career, the big house, the big car, the big *life*. It all came at a price, though. There was a divorce; though she's remarried now and loving her empty nest, there were hard years when she'd come over and cry from the sheer exhaustion of juggling everything. I came to understand that there is no such thing as a perfect life, just a constant shifting, like the wind on the lake. You adjust your sails to catch the wind, not the other way around.

I often wonder, if I'd stuck with my degree program, would I have found my passion? That first semester, I floundered, unable make up my mind. I had friends who were so clear-eyed, wanting to be a kindergarten teacher. Or a CPA. Or a landscape designer. Not me. I never quite found the right fit. Skipping college, setting aside the thought of a professional career, turned out well for me. Life is good enough. We wanted more kids, but because of that female problem, which turned out to be not so little, it was not to be.

As each mile brings Molly and me closer to goodbye, I realize how little I know about this rarefied world she is about to enter. I wonder if it will drive a wedge between us, turn her into a stranger to me, a sophisticated stranger with a big vocabulary and bigger dreams. There won't be any three o'clock bell to start my world turning again. No swing to push in the backyard, no cookies to bake.

What there *will* be is time. So much of it. All the time in the world to figure out what to do with my life, now that I can do anything I want. This should not feel so fraught with uncertainty. Parents have done this since time immemorial. Fretting about it is silly.

I'm not fretting, that's the thing. I'm *afraid*.

We argue about where to spend the night. Should we stop on the west side of Omaha, or try to make it to the east side by nightfall, thus avoiding tomorrow's morning rush of inbound traffic?

"I'd just as soon stop now," I declare, checking the dashboard clock. "We're making good enough time."

Molly wants to keep driving. She has an adolescent's inexhaustible supply of late-night energy combined with an eagerness to get there. "Forget it," she says. "I'm going past the city for sure. No need to cut the day short."

"Come on, Moll—"

"I'm driving, Mom. You said I could. That means I get to pick where we stop. Find a stopping place in the Triple-A guide and pick a motel."

For a moment, I feel disoriented. Who is this person in the driver's seat, telling me what to do? A small laugh erupts from me.

"What's funny?" asks Molly.

"You sound like your mother."

"And that surprises you?"

"Yes. A little. I guess." Bemused, I take out the Triple-A

guide. It is something I recall from my own childhood. We used to go on grim road trips each summer, with me and my three siblings fighting in the backseat, our dad hunched doggedly over the steering wheel and our mom flipping pages in the triptych while reciting facts and figures from the guidebook.

"Grady, Nebraska. Population 4,500," I tell Molly now. "There are four possible motels, two with two-diamond ratings and two with three."

"Go for the three."

Finally, something we agree on.

Chapter Four

We make our way to the Star Lite Motor Court and Coffee Shop. I'm not sure what the three diamonds in the auto guide signify. There's a pool, but a suspicious-looking green tinge stains the tiles, so Molly and I decide against taking a swim. The coffee shop looks promising; it's open late, and features a grill hissing with frying burgers, and a revolving glass case displaying pies of mythic proportions.

We let ourselves into our room, wondering what three-diamond amenities we'll find there. The carpet smells faintly of mildew and ancient cigarettes, so we open a window to let in fresh air. Ugh, I think with a twinge of disappointment. Given the nature of this journey, I'd hoped for better accommodations. I'd pictured the two of us sharing a charming suite in a B&B, or working out in the fitness room of a modern hotel. As usual, there's a gap between expectation and reality.

Molly flings herself on one of the beds, bouncing happily. "I love road trips," she crows. "I love staying in motels."

And with that, the disappointment is gone, lifted away by the grin on her face. I am forced to notice this small but significant shift. Molly's mood has the power to determine my own. This was never apparent when she was at home, but once she's gone, where will the happiness come from? I need to make sure I remember how to find it.

"What's this?" She indicates the metal Magic Fingers box on the nightstand.

"You've never heard of Magic Fingers?"

"What?"

"Move over." I dig some quarters out of my jeans pocket, drop them in the slot and lie down next to Molly. "Your education's not complete until you've experienced Magic Fingers."

Nothing happens. "I guess it's broken," I say. "The thing is probably thirty years old if it's a day."

"Just because it's old doesn't mean it's broken." Determined, Molly reaches across me and gives the box a shake. Still nothing. She messes with the cord. And then: "Whoa. Did you feel that?"

I lie very still. There is a mechanical hum, then a faint vibration buzzes upward, penetrating through me and increasing in strength. Molly relaxes next to me, supine.

"Okay," she says. "This is weird."

"It'll stop in a few minutes."

"Weird in a good way," she amends.

"I can't believe you never tried this before." Through the years, we've stayed in dozens of motels together but this is the first time we've found Magic Fingers. "I guess they're a thing of the past," I tell her.

"Good thing we decided to stop here, huh?" She sighs with contentment.

A kinder way of saying "I told you so." We lie side by side, the bed humming beneath us for long minutes. When the vibrations stop, I am startled to feel more relaxed, the rigors of the long driving day eased from my muscles.

"What are you thinking about?" Molly asks.

The question catches me off guard. "You, I suppose. I've always liked doing new things with you, even little things."

"Like Magic Fingers."

"Exactly. Everything was new with you. That's what was so much fun about raising a child. I'd be in the middle of doing something—whipping egg whites into meringue or riding my bike with no hands or graphing a parabola—and you'd think I was amazing. A magician or something."

"You *were* amazing," Molly says quietly, turning on her side and tucking her hand under her cheek.

I must be hearing things. I consider asking her to say that again, but I doubt she will repeat it. "Who will I amaze now that you're leaving?"

Molly laughs. "Excuse me?"

"I'm losing my audience."

"You should have had more kids," she observes.

I hesitate, caught off-guard by her words. Yet not off-guard at all. It's an opening to a difficult conversation. I know this before either of us speaks again.

"Mom?"

I turn to her. "I couldn't have any more babies after..."

Her eyes widen. "After you had me?"

I gaze into her face, seeing maturity and wisdom there, trusting the compassion in her expression. When I first conceived of this cross-country adventure, I knew things would come up between us, difficult matters. And I knew this matter was the most difficult of all. Through the years, I had protected Molly from the most painful episode of my life. It wasn't fair to reveal a wound she didn't cause and couldn't heal. What would be the point of that?

Things are different now. She's a young woman. Another person's pain won't confuse or destroy her. Isn't that, after all, the essence of maturity?

Deep breath, I tell myself, gazing into her doe-soft eyes. "I had a baby boy named Bruce." Even after so much time has passed, I still feel the piercing loss. I was bleeding, drugged half out of my mind, but I can feel him even now, his slight, unmoving weight in my arms. Weeks premature, he was as pale and beautiful and silent as a fallen angel, having never drawn breath in this world.

Molly's eyes instantly fill with tears. "Mom, really? What happened? When?"

Pulling in a deep breath, I explain in a shaky voice. "You were just two years old at the time. He came too early, and I was bleeding. There was a tear in my uterus."

"Oh, Mom. Why didn't you ever tell me?"

I feel a tear slide over the bridge of my nose. Such an old, old wound, made fresh again by indelible memories. When it happened, it changed me in ways I am still discovering, even now. That kind of loss has the power to stop the world. My baby boy's tiny, other-worldly face will always haunt me. He looked so very much like my other newborn, Molly. "It was just so sad, honey."

She reaches for me and we're quiet together for a long time, the moments slipping by, measured by our breathing.

"I don't know what to say," she whispers.

"You don't have to say anything." There are some things that simply can't be made better, not by talking or weeping or praying or pretending they didn't happen. Yet her reaction is exactly as I'd hoped it would be—compassionate without being pitying or obsessive.

"I wish…" Her voice trails off, but I understand exactly what she's saying.

"So do I."

More quiet moments. We turn on the Magic Fingers again to shake us out of the somber mood. "You're all the kid I need," I tell her. She's heard that from me before. Now she understands the hidden meaning behind the words.

"Well, I hope you know, I'm the one losing my audience," Molly insists. "When I'm away at college, who will *I* perform for?"

This surprises me. I know there are things she worries about, being so far from home in a strange world where no one knows her. Still, I thought her eagerness to go out and find her life had banished all her fears. Now I realize she's well aware of what she's leaving behind. And it's not just Travis Spellman. From her first smile to her last day of high school, and all the lost teeth, soccer trophies, piano recitals and Brownie badges in between, I've been there for her, cheering her on.

"I'll still be your number-one fan," I assure her.

"Sure, but it won't be the same." Then she smiles and bounces up off the bed.

I sit up and link my arms around my drawn-up knees. "You seem pretty okay with that."

"It's hard work, being your daughter."

"You're kidding, right?"

Now it's her turn to hesitate. "Right. Let's go check out the game room. I think I saw a ping-pong table."

Late at night, long after our dinner of iceberg lettuce salads and oyster crackers, Molly steals away to sit on the stoop in front of the motel room and call Travis on her cell phone. Although college beckons like a mysterious garden of rare delights, she has formed a deep bond with this boy, with his funny grin and Adam's apple, his appealing combination of cluelessness and charm.

A hometown boy at heart, he is causing her to have second thoughts about going to school so far away. For that, I could throttle him. At the same time, I feel an unexpected beat of empathy. I, too, would love to keep her close.

On their final night at home, Molly and Travis went out with a group of their friends, some college-bound, others already immersed in jobs and responsibilities. They stayed out late, visiting all the places they knew they'd miss after dispersing like seeds to the wind. There were stops at the rusty-screened drive-in movie theater, the empty stadium, the all-night diner, the parking lot at the spillway below the lake. I don't doubt there were other stops as well, which were not revealed to me.

I can't be certain, but I suspect that Molly surrendered her virginity at the spillway at some point during the summer, in the secret place known to revved-up teenagers everywhere, tucked into the shadows of the sloping man-made bank. She didn't tell me so, but there have been subtle signs. I've watched her and Travis grow closer, their bond tightened by a private and impenetrable intimacy that is both invisible and obvious.

Sexually active. It's a clinical-sounding term. It's nothing a mother wants to think about with regard to her own child, but at some point, you have to take the blinders off. Or not, I suppose, thinking of Dan. Whenever I try to bring the subject up with him, he says, "They're good kids. They won't do anything stupid."

Pointing out that good kids who are not stupid get in trouble all the time doesn't seem to advance the conversation. I have given up on discussing it with Dan. Now and then, I try to broach the topic with Molly.

"I'm *fine*. Don't worry," she said when I got up the nerve to ask her.

It doesn't matter what century we're in. Parents and children were not meant to talk together in detail about sex. Nor should we pretend to be all-knowing experts on love, even if we are. I understand exactly what love feels like in a young girl's heart because I was that girl once, long ago. That's why the Travis situation worries me, because I understand. It has a power like the pull of the moon on the tides, overwhelming and inevitable. There is no antidote for the passion and certainty a girl feels for the boy she loves, and no end to the fantasies she spins about their future together.

I can explain convincingly that the emotions engulfing her and Travis are not likely to last. I can tell her they'll both grow and change, heading off in different directions. But then I would have to talk about my own choices, my own regrets, the many times I spent wondering about the life I would have had if I'd taken a different path.

For a brief moment, I consider telling Molly about Preston Warner, my first and, as far as I was concerned at the time, my only, forever and ever. Senior prom was the kind of magic-filled night every girl dreams about and, in my case, the dream came true. I wore something blue and silky; Preston was slicked-down, tux-clad and nervous. Not only did we consummate our relationship that night, we pledged to stay true forever, even though Preston was going far away to college.

That night, I surrendered not just my virginity but all my hopes and dreams, handing them over to a boy who— though I didn't realize it at the time—had no idea what to do with them. So he did what guys his age generally do. Three months into his first semester at a trendy private school a day's drive away, he started dating other people. When I found out, I wanted to die. I walked around like a zombie, every bit of happiness having bled from my broken heart.

I still remember the drama of our final confrontation— he came in person to tell me it was over. To this day, I can still feel the horror of facing a future without him. I raged, I wept until I was weak and drained, I swore I could not go on. It caused a pain I couldn't share with anyone. My mother brought me a pint of Cherry Garcia, but I promised her I'd never eat again. She said with utter confidence that I'd get over him. Then she went downstairs and ironed clothes, filling the house with the scent of lavender water. I ate the Cherry Garcia. Watched *Seinfeld* reruns and learned

to laugh again. Somehow, one day dragged into the next…
and eventually I realized that I didn't miss him.

Hearing a heartbroken sniffle and the murmur of Molly's
voice drifting through the window screen of the motel, I
decide not to tell her any of that. She and Travis will grow
apart because that's the way it works. She will have to find
this out for herself. The end of love has to be experienced
firsthand, not explained by your mother.

I turn on the radio to give her more privacy. Even so, I
can guess what they're saying. There are whispered promises
of love-you-forever and we'll-stay-together, and no one
knows as well as I do that they mean it—every word. Preston and I certainly meant it, all those years ago. We were
going to travel the world and live a charmed life together.

These days, Preston owns the hardware store in town and
has a cushy paunch around his middle, a receding hairline
and four kids. When I drop in to buy upholstery tacks or
a can of paint, I always think about that last summer after
high school, the passionate hours in the backseat of his car,
the vows we made to each other. I can look past his bifocals
and graying temples, and still see a boy who was as handsome and romantic as a fairy-tale prince. As Preston rings
up my purchases and we make small talk, I wonder if he
thinks about the way we were, too, if he remembers. Does
he look at me in my pull-on slacks and gardening clogs and
recall the girl I used to be?

Running into him is, weirdly enough, not awkward in
the least. He's someone who came into my life for a brief
time, and then stayed in the past. I feel no wistfulness for
him, no regrets. I do envy him those four kids, though.

When one goes away, he still has the others to keep him company.

Or maybe saying goodbye four times is harder than saying it once.

When Molly comes back into the room, her eyes red and her chin trembling, I offer a smile, but I don't say anything. This is a volatile issue, and I don't want to push it. Travis is a boy of good looks and small ambition, one who regards his union job at the plant as a ticket to independence as well as an opportunity to work on his Camaro at his uncle's garage on the weekends.

Travis has a peculiar sweetness about him, a quality Molly finds irresistible. She loves him, and her love is as real as her grade point average. She trusts that love to endure, no matter what.

Molly expects so much of herself and wants so much from the world. At the moment, she is tender and lonely, missing him, her heart sore as it can only be for one's first love.

I have to wonder: Did I teach my daughter to love this hard and feel this deeply? Was I wrong to do so? On the other hand, maybe I shielded her too much from pain, and she never learned to deal with it. As more men loom in the future, a whole campus full of them, it makes me wonder if I've done enough to equip her to deal with love and heartache. My own mother never seemed comfortable discussing matters of the heart with me. That's what I used to think, anyway. Now I wonder if she simply knew I'd discover it all for myself.

"Hungry?" I ask Molly, after she's lain on the bed, staring at the ceiling for a while. "The coffee shop's still open."

"No," she says softly. "You?"

"No." This is a lie. The dinner salad was a disappointment. But I don't need to eat. I don't need that big, messy cheeseburger I've been fantasizing about since spotting it on the coffee-shop menu. I don't need the coconut cream pie I noticed in the revolving refrigerated case. Something my mother never told me—when you hit forty, not only does your vision start to go. Your body changes. Nowadays if I eat things like cheeseburgers and cream pie, the calories magically transform themselves into saddlebags on my hips. I don't feel any different than I did ten years ago, but boy, do my jeans fit differently.

My mind drifts. Maybe when I get home, I'll join the local gym, start a regular fitness routine. Running around with Molly has kept me reasonably fit all these years. Thanks to her, I've hiked miles with Brownie and Girl Scout troops, led field-trip expeditions to museums or nature preserves, ridden for hours on family bike trips. I suppose I could still hike and bike without Molly around, but why would I? Motivating myself is not going to be as easy as it used to be.

A quiet sniff brings me back to the present. I look over at Molly to see that she is still staring at the ceiling. Tears track sideways down her temples.

I don't say anything, because I know everything will come out sounding like empty platitudes. Instead, I find another quarter, drop it in the slot and start up the Magic Fingers once again.

Day Three

Odometer Reading 122,271

" It is not wise to be didactic about
the nomenclature of quilt patterns."
—Florence Peto, *American Quilts and Coverlets* (1949)

"...it is unwise to be didactic
because the facts are very elusive.
I now realize that not every
pattern has a name, that there is
no correct name for any design."
—Barbara Brackman, *Encyclopedia of Pieced Quilt Patterns*

Chapter Five

The roadside is littered with last night's carnage, a raccoon here, a possum there, occasionally someone's household pet reduced to an unrecognizable smear. Neither Molly nor I say a word. I hate the idea of creatures suffering while people sleep, oblivious.

This morning's breakfast—the Bright Eyes Surprise, which I'd ordered solely because I liked the name—churns in my stomach. From the driver's seat, Molly reaches over and turns up the radio. She glides into the passing lane to get around a semi with a tweeting cartoon robin on the side.

I refold the map to encompass the day's journey. We plan to make tracks today, covering at least four hundred miles. The few towns along the way are no more than pinpricks with quirky names, like Nickel Box and Mulehorn and Futch's Corner. Mostly, it appears we'll be crossing uninhabited terrain, much of it protected by the Department of Natural Resources, shaded in green.

"Do we have plenty of gas?" I ask.

"Three quarters of a tank. Same amount we had the last time you asked, ten minutes ago."

The biggest of the pinpricks, Futch's Corner, lies at the halfway point. We'll get gas there.

"I can't decide whether to quilt or read," I tell Molly.

"Why don't you listen to music and look at the scenery?"

"I already did that."

She laughs a little, shakes her head. "You always have to be busy doing something."

"Nothing wrong with that."

"Except you might miss something. Chill, Mom."

"All right. I'll look out the window." The most interesting thing I spot is a red-winged blackbird in a thicket of cattails.

If I'm being honest with myself, there's a reason for staying busy. Being preoccupied with other things means I don't have to be preoccupied with my own baggage. I'm sick of myself, of my indecisiveness and mental whining. My daughter's leaving the nest, as all daughters eventually do, and my job is to let her go and move on with my life. It should be a simple matter to set a goal for myself, one that doesn't involve Molly, even indirectly. Maybe I don't have a college degree, but I'm not stupid.

I know I have to figure out who I am again, now that I'm not Molly's mom. Well-meaning friends tell me to go back to being the person I was before Molly. Am I that twentysomething woman who used to sleep late and smoke Virginia Slims and never felt the need to look at a clock?

That's not me anymore. It can never be me again. I don't want to go back to being that person who lived each day so thoughtlessly, spending the moments like nickels in a slot machine, as though she had an unending supply of time and could squander it any way she pleased.

Other friends remind me that my marriage moves to the front burner now. Dan and I will have to figure out how to be a childless couple again. What were we before we became Molly's parents? What did we used to talk about, dream about, laugh and cry about? A better stereo system, a bigger house, an extra week's vacation from work? How could those things matter now?

It was Molly who showed us the things that matter most. They're the moments that sneak up on you unexpectedly, when you're barely paying attention. You're going out to see if the mail has come, and you discover that your child has learned to ride a two-wheeler and is as thrilled about it as if she's learned to fly. Or you uncrate the new refrigerator you scrimped and saved for, and she shows you that the best thing about the new appliance is the empty box.

Before Molly, what was it that mattered to Dan and me? When we were first married, he'd grab me the second he woke up each morning and say, "You're here!" as if I were the answer to his dreams. I can't remember when he stopped doing that. Granted, it would seem tedious and downright weird if he kept it up indefinitely, but there was a clear appeal in knowing exactly where I stood with him.

Inside the oval hoop is a swatch of my mother's favorite cotton blouse, the one with tiny umbrellas printed all over it. For some reason, I'm inspired to stitch a message: "Do the thing you fear."

Not the thing your mother fears. The thing *you* fear. I hope Molly will understand the difference.

Something extraordinary flashes past my line of sight. "Molly, slow down," I say. "Look over there."

It's a turnoff marked Leaning Tower of Pisa, Iowa.

"Let's check it out," I say.

Molly looks dubious. Her gaze flicks to the dashboard clock. I feel a twinge of annoyance at her eagerness to reach our ultimate destination. Can't she slow down, just a little?

"You're the one who wanted me to watch the scenery and chill," I remind her. "We're making good time," I point out.

"All right. Let's do it."

We go take a look at the leaning tower, and it is exactly that. A water tower that has listed to one side. In the next big wind it could topple, explains a placard in the field beside it. We take pictures to email to Dan. We've been calling him to check in each day. The conversation is predictable—we're to keep the tank full and check the oil and tire pressure at least once a day. We're to take care of ourselves.

"See?" I try not to act too smug as we return to the car. "You learn something new every day."

Molly decides to give me a turn at the wheel. She wants to phone Travis and she's not allowed to do it while she's driving.

"No freakin' signal," she says, scowling at the screen of her cell phone. "That's lame."

"You'll just have to watch the scenery and chill."

She rummages in her bag and pulls out the folder of information sent to her by the college. "Kayla Jackson from Philadelphia," she says, referring to her roommate. "I wonder what she'll be like."

"Lucky," I say. "She was matched up with you, wasn't she?"

"Her mother's probably saying the same thing. Oh, man, what if we can't stand each other?"

"You said she sounded great in her email."

"Sex predators sound great in email, Mom."

My head whips in her direction. "How do you know that?"

"Everybody knows that. Geez, don't get your panties in a twist. I don't talk to perverts on email. I don't talk to perverts at all."

"Suddenly I feel as if we haven't discussed this topic enough."

"What, perverts? I'll talk about perverts anytime you want, Mom."

"All joking aside, honey—"

"Mom. We went through this a long time ago, the stuff about respecting myself and using my head. That women's self-defense class went on for twelve weeks and yes, I read *The Gift of Fear*. I'm as safe as it's possible to be."

"You have all the answers, don't you, Missy?"

"I'll have even more once I'm in college."

We stop for lunch and a fill-up in Futch's Corner, a town with four stoplights, a defunct train depot and a bus station. A row of storage silos covered in graffiti lines the main road. The lone café has a pictorial menu, which makes it easy to avoid the chopped salad, which in these parts appears to be coleslaw.

In the booth next to us, an elderly couple sits across from each other, slowly and methodically eating their cups of beef barley soup with soda crackers on the side. They manage to get through the entire meal without uttering a single word. The wife puts cream in both cups of coffee. When they get up after finishing their meal, the husband keeps one hand on the small of the wife's back.

"Old people are so cute, aren't they?" Molly remarks.

Old people are a nightmare. It's too easy for me to see myself and Dan in a couple like that, silent and companionable, with nothing to say to each other. I want so much more for us, laughter and interesting conversation, the richness of shared moments. I used to think I knew what my life would look like after Molly, but now I'm not so sure.

Once she's away at school, Dan and I are going to have to face each other once again with nothing between us, no sports matches to attend, no carpools to drive, no curfews to enforce, no school calendar to dictate our lives. To me, it looks like a void, a yawning breach. Empty space. It's supposed to be a good thing, but I've never been the sort to tolerate empty space. Maybe that's why I like quilting. Each piece fits perfectly against the others to fill the grid completely.

On the highway heading east again, we come upon a breakdown pulled off to the side of the road. I slow down but don't stop. The hood of the car is raised and there's a woman standing beside it. She has a baby on her hip and there's no one else in sight. I go even slower, checking the rearview mirror, hoping to see that she's on a cell phone, getting help.

She isn't. She's jiggling the baby and taking a diaper bag out of the car.

Someone else will come along and help her, I figure. But this is a lonely stretch of highway and there's no one in sight in either direction.

"What are you doing?" Molly asks when I stop and make a U-turn.

"Making sure that woman back there is okay. Maybe she needs my cell phone."

"Mom. Aren't you the one with all the rules about not picking up strangers?"

"I didn't say anything about picking her up. But I'm not going to leave her stranded." I pass the breakdown, pull another U-turn and park on the shoulder in front of the woman's car, a dusty Chevy Vega with Nevada plates.

"Thanks for stopping," she says. "I blew a radiator hose." She doesn't appear to be much older than Molly. She's wearing a man's ribbed tank top under an open shirt, shorts and flip-flops. Her eyes are puffy and the baby is fussing.

"Have you called for help?"

"I don't have a phone and the last town's forty miles back."

"Let's try my cell phone," I offer, getting out of the car and handing it to her.

The baby glowers at me. It's a boy, maybe fourteen months, and he smells like ripe fruit. His nose is running green sludge, and he has a rattling cough. As his mother dials the phone, he pokes a grubby finger at the buttons.

"Nothing," she says after a moment. "No signal. Thanks

anyway." She hands back the phone. I resist the urge to clean it off on my shirttail.

The baby barks out a cough. The woman looks around. A breeze shimmers through the silver maples and a few dry leaves fall off, scattering. There is a folded umbrella stroller and a car seat in the back of the car.

The silence stretches out. I take a deep breath, violating my own better judgment as I say, "We'll give you a ride."

"You don't have to do that." Despite her words, the woman looks as if she might melt with relief.

Molly gets out of the car, map in hand. The cranky baby glowers at her.

"Really, you don't," the woman persists.

"It's fine," I assure her. "Where are you headed?"

"Honeymoon," she says. "It's my hometown. I'm moving back there, but this piece of crap car doesn't want to cooperate."

Molly finds the town on the map. It's about fifty miles to the north on a road marked with a faint gray line, well out of our way. The smart thing to do would be to drive on until I get a cell phone signal and then call in the location of the breakdown.

Maybe I'm not so smart. I keep thinking if Molly were stranded, I'd want a nice woman to stop. "Molly, can you give me a hand with the baby's car seat?" I ask.

My daughter's eyebrows lift, but she instantly complies.

I introduce myself and learn that the woman's name is Eileen. Her baby is Josten. "His grandparents have never seen him," she says. "I sure appreciate this." Wrinkling her nose, she adds, "He needs a change." She lays him on the backseat of her car. The creases of the seat are filled with bits of broken cookies and dry cereal. "Last one," she says, extracting a diaper from the bag.

The little one yowls as she peels off his romper and diaper. "Cut it out," she snaps as he kicks at her. "Josten—oh, Josten. What a mess." She digs in the diaper bag. "Shoot. I'm out of baby wipes."

Molly looks on in horror for a moment, then grabs something from the quilt bag. "Here, use this."

It's a piece of an old Christmas tree skirt from Dan's and my first Christmas together. You can't really tell it was ever a tree skirt; it just looks like a green tablecloth.

"Are you sure?" Eileen asks.

"No problem," I tell her.

"Thanks."

Molly's expression is priceless as she watches Eileen dry the kid's tears and wipe his nose, then clean his bottom. This is a better justification for birth control than any lecture from me, although it means a sad end for the old tree skirt. Eileen puts on a clean diaper, but the romper is soaked through. The baby starts wailing again.

"I don't have a change of clothes for him." Eileen looks like she's about to lose it, too.

I glance at the quilt bag, hesitating only a moment. At the bottom is a pair of Oshkosh overalls in candy pink. "This will probably work. It was Molly's when she was about his size. See if it fits." I answer the question in her expression. "I brought along a bag of old fabric scraps to add to the quilt I've been working on."

"Then I can't take this."

"Sure, go ahead. I've got plenty. I have enough."

She threads him into the overalls. The baby cries as she

straps him into his car seat, the sobs punctuated with liquid coughs. Eileen gives him a plastic bottle of Gerber apple juice, but he flings it away. Molly is actively trying not to cringe; I can tell.

"Hush," Eileen says. "Please. Sorry about him."

"You don't need to apologize. Is he running a fever?"

"A little, I think. I gave him some Tylenol drops right before you stopped." She loads in the diaper bag and her purse, then locks her car, and we all take off.

Eventually, the storm of crying subsides as the monotony of the ride lulls the baby. The stretch of road that looked so innocent on the map is narrow and curving, with a posted speed limit of forty. It's too late to change our minds now, though. We're committed.

We learn that Eileen and her boyfriend went to Vegas together to get work. "My mother didn't want me to leave, but there was nothing for me in Honeymoon, except maybe some crap job at a fast-food place. Vegas was our best bet, especially since I wanted to be a dancer. I *was* a dancer, until I got pregnant."

"Onstage, in Vegas?" Molly turns to her in interest.

Eileen nods her head. "I was in the chorus line of a show at the Monte Carlo."

"That's so cool," Molly says.

"It was. But...harder than you'd think, especially with a kid and a lousy boyfriend. My mother danced, too, but never professionally. She always wanted to work onstage and didn't ever have the chance."

"Then it's great that you got the opportunity," I tell her, trying to say something positive.

Eileen gives a brief, humorless laugh. "I doubt my mother

would think so. She was scared I might succeed at something she never got to do."

I have no idea what to say to this. I peek in the rearview mirror. Eileen is stroking the hair off Josten's forehead. "Mama tried like hell to talk me out of going, but I went anyway," she says. "Big mistake."

"What, leaving home?" Molly asks.

"Leaving with *him*. With my boyfriend, Mick. My ex, now."

There is no air of I-told-you-so when we stop at a modest clapboard house at the far side of a town called Honeymoon. Eileen's mother, who doesn't look a day over forty, gathers her into a hug that emanates relief and gratitude. She inspects the baby, now groggy and mellow from his nap, and holds him against her as if he's a missing piece of herself. "Look at this doll baby," she whispers, shutting her eyes and inhaling. "Just look at him."

Through the lines of fatigue around her mouth, Eileen beams. "It's good to be home," she says.

"I'm glad you're here," the mother replies. "No idea what I did without you." Then she turns and thanks me in a trembling voice. "Would you like to stay for supper?" she asks. "I got some sweet corn from a neighbor. And I just made some lemonade, fresh."

"Thanks, but we have to keep going," I tell her.

Molly surprises me by saying, "Maybe a glass of lemonade…"

The woman, whose name is Shelley, serves it in mismatched glasses and asks us about our trip.

"My mom's dropping me off at college," Molly says.

"Goodness, college. That's exciting."

The baby starts fussing himself awake and Eileen turns away to tend to him. I admire the patchwork quilt draped over the back of the sofa, and Shelley tells me it's a family heirloom.

"I'm working on one myself," I say. "It's my biggest project to date."

"I like sewing," she says. "I made all of Eileen's costumes for her dance routines. I don't sew much anymore. The local fabric store folded, and the nearest superstore's thirty miles away. They got everything you need there, but I miss the shop. All the women were friends, you know?"

I think of the shop back home. Here in the middle of nowhere, this woman had nailed it—a community for women.

She gives us a local map that shows more detail than my Triple-A triptych. She indicates a route back to the highway that will put us a good eighty miles ahead of where we were.

Molly takes over driving again. I pick up my quilting. She says, "Dad's going to freak when you tell him we picked up a stranger."

"She needed a lift. We had no choice."

"I'm glad we helped her out. We're behind on our schedule now, though."

"We don't need to be anywhere specific," I note. "It was a goal, the four hundred miles."

We drive through a few towns fringed by strip malls or trailer parks. There is an air of exhaustion that seeps into the atmosphere of these places, and we're glad to leave them behind.

By the time we reach the highway, dusk has fallen and it's

time to find food and a place to spend the night. An eerie emptiness hovers over the open road and few cars pass by.

"It's looking bleak," Molly says. "How far to the next city?"

"Almost a hundred miles. You up for it?"

"Looks like we don't have a choice."

She plugs an adaptor into her iPod so we can listen on the stereo speakers, and we get into a discussion about the stupidest lyrics ever written—"This Is Why I'm Hot" would be my pick. But Molly points out Van Morrison's "Ringworm" and then we dissect the lyrics of some old Yes songs.

"Anything sounds stupid if you listen too closely," I say.

Molly switches to a track that's in French. "Clearly, we've been in the car together too long."

A few minutes later, I spot a billboard rising from an alfalfa field, with a light shining on it. "Ramblers Rest, in Possum, Illinois. Want to check it out?"

She nods and drives another mile to the next sign. There's a red-neon light indicating Vacancy in the window of the office, which also contains a convenience store. The tires crackle over the gravel in the drive.

"What do you think?" Molly asks.

"It's worth a look. If it's horrible, we'll drive away."

It's not horrible, just a bit strange. Ramblers Rest consists of a group of small, self-contained wayfarers' cabins at the edge of a small trout pond. Our room is plain but clean, with walls of scrubbed pine, checkered curtains and an old-fashioned prayer posted above one of the beds.

The proprietor, a man in jeans and a plaid shirt, tells us there's a bonfire down by the pond where guests gather around to sing songs and toast marshmallows.

"Songs?" Molly mutters. "No way."

"We could harmonize 'You Are My Sunshine.'"

She cringes, and I send her a wicked grin. "Or 'Kumbaya'?"

The closest restaurant, our host says, is a place called Grumpy's, a few miles down the road.

"They're probably closed now," he warns.

Starving, we head up to the convenience shop adjacent to the office and buy hot dogs to roast over the fire, plus bright yellow mustard and squishy white buns—the kind of meal that is forbidden in a proper kitchen. On a whim, I buy the ingredients for a kind of dessert we haven't made since Molly's childhood camping trips. We hike down to the water's edge where a teepee-shaped bonfire roars at the night sky. There are at least three discrete groups here, but all share that sort of instant camaraderie that seems to crop up among strangers at campgrounds. They make room for us in the firelit circle and we roast hot dogs, sharing the extras.

It's amazingly tranquil around the pond, the sky intensely black in the absence of city lights. It's so dark you can make out the colors of the stars—red and violet, silver and the shimmering green of moss in shadow. Their reflections glow like coins on the surface of the water.

Molly and I sit shoulder-to-shoulder and make small talk with the other travelers. There's a young family from Cottage Grove, who just sold their house and are moving to Cleveland. A not-so-young family is there, too. The parents are about my age, but the kids are little, with Asian features, so I assume they're adopted. A retired couple, who seem self-contained and not as eager to mingle, tell us they're on a monthlong driving tour of the midwest. Molly, of course, gravitates toward two boys who seem to be about her age. They're juniors at Penn State, so leaving home is routine to them, and they're driving themselves.

She seems to have forgotten about dessert, but the younger kids eagerly gather around when I ask them if they want to help. I demonstrate how to put a little whipping cream and sugar into a small Ziploc bag. The sealed bag then goes into a larger plastic bag of ice and salt. This is the kids' favorite part—you shake until the cream and sugar in the sealed bag turns to ice cream.

"What a great trick," the young mother says to me, watching her little ones shiver and shake.

"I learned it from my mother." I look across at Molly, who is now explaining the process to the college boys, who are totally into it. Before long, everyone around the campfire is making ice cream in a bag, the kids turning it into a wild dance. Sparks land on someone's blanket, and a tiny flame ignites. Fortunately, it is spotted and beaten out. People tuck their loose blankets away from the fire, and we're more vigilant after that.

Everyone pronounces the ice cream delicious. In fact, it's a bit bland, but flavored by the fun we had making it. One of the college boys plays a harmonica. Then, possessed by the silliness of knowing we'll never see these people again, Molly and I sing "You Are My Sunshine" in perfect harmony, and our listeners are polite enough to clap. We stay by the fire way too late, until I feel the stiffness of the long day and the cold night at my back.

"I'm heading to bed," I tell Molly. I worry that she might want to linger here with the college boys. Her eyes glow when she talks to them. I battle the urge to remind her that these guys are strangers and we're in a strange place. Pretty soon, I won't be around to protect her at all, so I'd best get used to the churning nervousness in my gut.

She surprises me by getting up and helping collect the trash and leftovers. "I'm going to turn in, too. If we get an early start, we can make up for the time we lost today."

We didn't lose any time. I know exactly how and where we spent it, and I wouldn't change a thing.

As we walk together to our cabin, Molly says, "Those kids loved making the ice cream."

"Remember the first time I made it with you?"

"The Brownie campout at Lake Pegasus. I was—what— six years old? And I had the coolest mom."

What I remember about that campout was feeling inadequate. The professional moms, as I'd come to regard them, had remembered everything from bug spray to breakfast bars. They knew how to roast a whole meal in a foil packet, braid a lanyard into a friendship bracelet and name the constellations. My clever little ice cream trick didn't seem like much. Now I'm ridiculously pleased to know she thought I was the coolest.

Molly goes off to shower. I flip through the Triple-A book, wondering what tomorrow will bring. On the back cover is an ad I never noticed before, with a list of phone numbers—who to call in event of a breakdown.

Odometer Reading 122,639

"As her father and brother constructed the simple, sturdy shelter that might house generations after her, a young girl at her mother's knee would work her own Log Cabin. It became the quintessential American quilt."

—Sandi Fox,
Small Endearments, 19th Century Quilts for Children

Chapter Six

The next day we make tracks and we're curiously quiet with one another, both lost in our private worlds and lulled by the monotony of the road. We stop for the night at a far more conventional place, one with wireless internet and pay-per-view movies. We are not nearly as entertained by this as we were by last night's bungalows and campfire. The room smells of new carpet and cleaning solution. The beds are like two rectangular rafts, covered in beige spreads.

"Let's go out," I say, opening the door to the parking lot to scan the neon collage of signs along the main drag.

Molly looks at me as if I've sprouted horns. "What do you mean, out? We already had dinner."

"I mean out. To one of these clubs."

"And do what?"

I have to think for a minute. It's been a long time since I've gone to a club. "Get something to drink," I explain. "I'm sure bartenders still remember how to make a Shirley Temple. We can people-watch and listen to music."

"What if I get carded?"

"It's legal for you to be in a bar in Ohio so long as you aren't served."

"You checked?"

"I always check."

She looks so dubious that I feel vaguely insulted. "What?"

"It's just weird going clubbing with your mom."

"We're not going clubbing. We're going to a club, just to get out a little bit. Nothing else seems to be open."

"That's weird."

"Fine. Let's stay here. You can watch *Simpsons* reruns and I'll work on the quilt and reminisce about the past."

Fifteen minutes later, we're headed out the door. Molly spent the entire preparation time in front of the mirror. I have to admit, she has a knack for primping. Her eyes are now smoky around the edges, her hair glossy and her lips slick and pink. She gives me the once-over and frowns again.

"I've seen that shirt before, Mom."

"I never realized you *noticed* this shirt before." I smooth my hands down the polished cotton. Except it's not so polished anymore. I think the polish wore off some time ago.

"Isn't it kind of...old?"

"It still fits. It's in perfectly good shape."

"But you've had it forever. Those jeans, too, and the shoes. And the purse. You carried that purse when you drove first-grade carpool."

"I take care of my belongings," I explain. "It's a virtue."

"Sure, but...Mom? You keep things too long."

She speaks kindly, yet I know what she's saying. Although I've always been quick to get something new for

Molly, I never paid much attention to my wardrobe. Other than the occasional school event, I don't tend to need much in the way of clothes. I can sew like the wind, but I like doing costumes and crafts, not blouses and shifts. And I've never been much for shopping. I laugh at Molly as I grab a light jacket and my purse. "Trust me, the world is not interested in my lack of style sense. Especially not when I'm with a girl who's flaunting her midriff."

"I'm not flaunting." She checks out her cropped shirt in the mirror.

A year ago, she had begged us to let her get a tattoo and, of course, we refused. Once she turned eighteen, she didn't need our permission but, to my immense relief, she didn't run out to the tattoo parlor. Maybe she forgot it was the one thing that was going to make her life complete. I'm not about to remind her.

We walk out together into the twilight, and the breeze holds just the faintest hint of the coming fall. There's none of the coolness of autumn in it, but a nearly ineffable dry scent. The smell of something just past ripeness.

The main street is lined with mid-twentieth-century buildings of blond brick or cut stone. The shops and banks are closed, window shades pulled like half-lidded eyes, but in the center of the block, the sound of music and laughter streams from three different clubs.

One of them, called Grins, has a sandwich board out front boasting No Cover. Across the street is Tierra del Fuego, featuring unspecified live music, and two doors down is a place called Home Base. Twinkling lights surround a picture of Beulah Davis, and we choose that club because she has the same last name as us and because I like her picture. She's smiling, though there's a wistful look in her eyes. Her hands, draped over an acoustic guitar, look strong, capable of bearing the weight of a large talent.

We enter between sets. Canned music pulsates from hidden speakers. The place is crowded with people clustered around bar-height tables. The yeasty scent of beer hangs in the air. A group of guys is playing pool under a domed light with a Labatts insignia. In the corner, the musical set is dark and quiet, two guitars—acoustic and steel—poised in their holders like wallflowers waiting to be asked for a dance.

I pause, letting my eyes adjust to the dimness, and a wave of uncertainty hits me. I can feel Molly's hesitation, too, and unthinkingly I grab her hand, still the mom, leading her to a booth that has a view of the dance floor and stage. A good number of couples are swaying in the darkness, the women's bare, soft arms draped around men's shoulders.

I miss Dan. It hits me suddenly, a swell of nostalgia. He's not fond of dancing, but he's fond of me. Sometimes he has no choice but to sweep me into his arms and dance with me.

Molly orders a 7UP with lime, and I ask for a beer on tap.

"I'll need to see some ID," the waitress says.

"The beer's for me."

"ID, please," she says, bending toward me.

This is both startling and flattering. I readily show her my driver's license; she nods in satisfaction and heads for the bar. Molly samples the snack mix and scans the crowd. It's a diverse bunch, people of all ages relaxing and talking, some of them drinking too much and laughing too loudly.

A couple in a booth across the room appears to be in an argument, leaning toward each other, their mouths twisted, ugly with overenunciated insults.

The music stops and the dancing couples fall still. The singer appears on the corner stage, accompanied by a drummer, a bass player and a woman on keyboard. Applause greets them and we set aside our drinks to listen. She picks up the steel guitar and smiles as they tune up, then places her lips close to the speakers. "Here's something by a guy I once knew, Doug Sahm, from Kilgore, Texas." A ringing, sweet melody slides from the speakers as she strokes the guitar.

It's the kind of song that sounds fresh, even though we've heard it a hundred times before. There's something about good live music that does that to a person. I feel a sense of happiness sprouting from within, and when I look across at Molly, I can tell that she feels it, too. There are very few people you can talk to without words. The fact that my daughter has always been one of those people for me is beyond price.

I grab and hang on to this moment, because I learned long ago that happiness is not one long, continuous state of being. Like life itself, happiness is made up of moments. Some are fleeting, lasting no longer than the length of a sweet song, yet the sum total of those moments can create a glow that sustains you. Watching Molly, I wonder if she knows that, and if she doesn't, if it's something I can teach her.

Sensing the question in my look, she tilts her head to one side and mouths, "Something wrong?"

The singer is joined by other band members, and the

set segues into a lively swing tune. The volume increases tenfold. I lean across the table. "Nothing's wrong. I'm just wondering if we've talked about what happiness is."

She cups her hand around her ear and her mouth moves again.

"Happiness," I say, nearly shouting. "Do you know how it works?"

She shakes her head, at a loss, then meets me halfway across the table. "Are you happy?" I ask in her ear.

She sits back down, laughing, and mouths the words, "I'm fine."

Her words remind me that there are some things I'm not meant to teach her. She'll only learn them by finding out for herself. I can hope and pray that I've raised a young woman who knows how to be happy, but I can't hand it to her like my mother's button collection, sealed in a mason jar. Starting now, she will have to be the steward of her own life.

After four songs, greeted with enthusiastic applause, the band takes a quick break and we buy a copy of their CD. The singer smiles a little bashfully and we smile back, two strangers who like the sound of her voice. She signs the case with an indelible marker. "Y'all enjoy that, now," she says.

"We will," I say.

The waitress reappears, another beer and another 7UP on her tray, even though we didn't ask for a second round.

"The gentlemen over there sent them," she explains, indicating with her thumb and a wink.

"Oh, uh…" My cheeks catch fire. I can't bring myself to look.

The waitress sets down the drinks and leaves.

"Get out of town," Molly says. "Mom, those guys sent us drinks."

"Don't make eye contact. And for heaven's sake, don't drink—"

She takes a sip of her fresh 7UP. Watching her expertly made-up eyes over the rim of the glass, I see a whole world of things I haven't told her, matters that need to be explained to someone who, in so many ways, is still only a child. I've had eighteen years to teach her not to accept gifts from strange men. I never got around to doing it. So much of this thing called parenting is a matter of waiting for a situation to arise and then addressing it. Just when you think you have all your bases covered, you—

"They're coming over," she says in a scandalized whisper.

I want to slither under the table. I've never been good in social situations, not with men, anyway. For Molly's sake I need to get over the urge to slither. This is a teachable moment.

"Thank you for the drinks," I tell the older one. He's maybe thirty, and the way he's looking at me makes me glad I'm wearing the mom clothes. "We were just leaving, though."

"I bet you have time for one dance," he says, smiling beneath a well-groomed mustache. He looks like the guy in that old TV series, *Magnum, P.I.* Magpie, Dan called it. I never did like that show.

His friend is clean-shaven, late twenties, checking out Molly with an expression that makes me want to call 911.

And here's the thing. I can't call 911. Nobody's doing anything illegal. It just feels that way to me.

"My mother and I really need to go," Molly says, polite

but firm as she stands up. She tugs her shirt down, probably hoping they don't notice her midriff.

"Just trying to be friendly," the clean-shaven one said. His buddy seems to be having a delayed reaction to the word *mother.*

On the way out, I hand the waitress $20 and don't ask for change.

"Okay, that was weird," Molly says as we step out onto the street.

"Honey, when a guy approaches you—"

"I didn't mean it was weird that they approached me," she interrupts. "I'm just not too keen on guys hitting on my mom."

"Guys hit on women. It's what they do. They don't think about whether she's somebody's mother. Or daughter, or sister. And when we were in there, all I could think about was whether or not I've talked to you enough about staying safe around strange guys."

She laughs. "You're killing me, Mom."

"Oh, that's right. You know everything. Sorry, I forgot." She doesn't realize it now, but the older she gets, the wiser *I* get.

Something I probably won't share with her—the last time I met a man in a bar, I married him. Not right away, of course. But there are eerie similarities. The bar was dim, like the one we just left, and—in those days—smoky. Dan didn't send a waitress to do his work for him. He strode right over to me and said, "Let me buy you a drink."

I was too startled to say no. By the time the drink arrived, it was too late. I had noticed his lanky height and merry eyes, the heft of his biceps and the humor in his voice and his mouth, even when he wasn't smiling. I wouldn't go so far as to say it was love at first sight, but it was definitely something powerful and undeniable.

He was a guy with clear potential and big plans, and I was a mediocre student at the state college. Less than half a year later, we found ourselves standing face-to-face at the altar, with nothing between us but dreams and candlelight. I still remember our first lowly, undemanding jobs and the way the days melted into a rhythm of partying every weekend, making love before dinner, staying up late and watching edgy movies.

Then Molly came along, and nothing was ever the same. We thought, at first, that nothing would change. Our denial ran deep; we walked around with her in a Snugli or stroller, pretending she was a fashion accessory.

Of course, she was so much more than that. She had the power to turn us into different people. We were no better and no worse, but different. She was our happiest, most blessed accident.

All of which goes to show what can happen when you talk to strange men in bars.

In the middle of the night, I wake up and blink at my surroundings, my sleep-blurred gaze tracking the seam of the drapes, glowing amber from the lights of the motel parking lot. I hear Molly breathing evenly, sweetly, a sound that catches at my heart now as it did the first time I ever heard it and thought, My God.

Emotion and memory chase away sleep and I get up, shuffling over to the laptop computer. I touch the keyboard and it wakes up, too. Little boxes tile the screen; Molly was

IMing with Travis late into the night. I quickly close the IM windows without reading the text.

It's 3:00 a.m., and the internet is there, waiting for me. Following the stream of my own thoughts, I click to site after site, surfing from link to link as though pulling myself along some invisible, unending chain. Ultimately, it's unsatisfying, filling my head with too much information. Yet it's given me a huge idea.

Slipping on a light jacket, I step out into the parking lot with my cell phone. The whole world is asleep. There are no cars on the street, no critters rooting in the trash, no breeze stirring the tops of the trees. I punch in our home number on the cell phone.

"It's me," I say when Dan picks up on the second ring.

"What?" he asks, grogginess burgeoning to panic. "Where the hell are you? Are you and Molly all right?"

"We're fine. We're in…" I think for a moment. "Ohio. She's sleeping."

"So what's the matter?" In Dan's book, if everything is fine with Molly, everything is fine, period. I can hear the bed creak, can picture him rolling over, pulling up the covers. "What time is it?"

I'm not about to tell him. "Late," I admit. "Sorry I woke you. I couldn't wait. Dan, I just thought of something."

"What did you think of, Lindy?" He never gets mad when I wake him up out of a sound sleep. I wonder how that can be. Suddenly I wish I was there with him, rubbing his warm shoulders with gentle persistence.

"We need to get an orphan."

"A what?"

"An orphan. You know, adopt a child."

"Huh?" Another creak of the bed, or maybe it's the sound of Dan, scowling.

"From Haiti."

"Linda, for Chrissake—"

"No, listen, I found this site on the internet. There are thousands of them, waiting for families. We have so much, Dan. We're still young. We could give some poor child a chance.

"There's one I found named Gilbert. He's six. He lost his family in the earthquake."

"Go back to bed, Linda. It was hard enough raising our own healthy, well-adjusted child."

"It hasn't been hard at all."

"Speak for yourself."

His comment reminds me of their struggles. His frustration, Molly's tears, the long silences and the breakdowns I used to feel compelled to fix. "We did a great job."

"I'm not saying we didn't. But we're done. It's our time now, Linda."

"And I want to do something with it, something that matters. Think about it, Dan. These kids…they're not sick or abused. They didn't grow up in institutions. They're kids like Molly, except they had the bad luck to come home from school one day to find that their families were gone."

"I'll send a check to the Red Cross."

"They need *families*. We could—"

"We could do a lot of things, but adopting an orphan from Haiti isn't one of them." He must know how that sounds, because he takes a breath and adds, "Honey, you're in panic mode over Molly leaving. This is no time to be discussing such a huge undertaking."

I pull the jacket tighter around me. Panic mode. Am I panicking?

"I need a child who needs me," I blurt out.

"Lindy. Slow down. What you need is a life of your own."

The words fall like stones on my heart. He's right. *He's right.* "I'll work on that," I say, feeling a bleak sweep of exhaustion.

"Have fun on your trip," Dan says, a yawn in his voice. "I love you both."

"Love you, too." After we hang up, I sit for a while and look at the stars. It's so quiet I can hear a train whistle blow, miles away.

DAY FIVE

Odometer Reading 123,277

"From the manner in which a woman
draws her thread at every stitch
of her needlework, any other woman
can surmise her thoughts."

—Honoré de Balzac

Chapter Seven

"I'm running out of thread," I tell Molly.

"We can stop somewhere in the next town," she says, unconcerned. She is more interested in finding a radio station. We have a rule. Driver gets to pick the music. We're already bored with our playlists and she's hungry for something new.

"This is mercerized thread spun from Sea Isle cotton," I explain. "It doesn't grow on trees, you know."

"I know how cotton is grown, Mom."

In quilting, the type and quality of thread you use matters greatly. Just think of all the stitches that go into a quilt. You need the kind of thread that pulls through smoothly, that is strong despite repeated tugging, that will never fray or pill.

To people who don't practice the craft of hand-sewing, thread is thread. Therefore, this is far less of a concern than the dearth of radio stations. The FM band yields too much

static, and the AM stations are crammed with crop reports
or the phony sentiment of country tunes.

"In pioneer days, mothers and daughters worked on their
quilts together," I tell her.

"Good thing we're not pioneers." A soybean rust update
comes on the radio, and she groans in exasperation.

I tried to get her interested in quilting a time or two, to
no avail. She was impatient with the detail and repetition.
Our few "lessons" ended with her pricking herself with
a needle and sighing loudly with boredom. She usually
wound up shooting baskets in the driveway with her dad.

She fiddles with the dial a bit more, and hits paydirt. The
announcer's voice says, "Settle back and enjoy this local
favorite, from Beulah Davis and the Strivers."

"Hey, isn't that the group we heard last night?" asks
Molly. "Cool."

The melody and words are soothing and emotional, and
I pause in the quilting to look out the window. It's a sea of
grass, rolling out on both sides, and I imagine Molly and
me as pioneers, setting off on a journey into the great, wide
unknown.

I wonder what it was like for those women and their
daughters, when their lives took them in different directions. They weren't able to pick up the phone or log onto
the internet and get in touch. Separation meant the possibility of never seeing each other again. I should count my
blessings.

The quilt section in my lap is made of cornflower-blue
fabric sprigged with tiny daisies. It was a dress I made for
Molly to wear to her very first piano recital, back when
she was just eight years old. Her first public performance.

What a nerve-wracking day that was. I recall her practicing Bach's "Minuet in G Major" over and over again until it drove Dan out into the yard with the weed-whacker. And I, of course, couldn't help tuning in on every note. I adjusted my breathing to the rhythm of her playing and when she hesitated—the long, agonizing pause in the fifth bar as she spread her tiny hand over the keys of a big chord—it made me hold my breath until she found the right notes. When she hit the wrong note I would wince and then remind myself not to do that at the recital.

The dress was meticulously put together, every stitch in place with hand-smocking across the bodice, the full skirt crisply ironed. She wore white ankle socks and Mary Janes, her hair held back in a blue band, and she looked like a dark-haired version of Alice in Wonderland.

"I'm not going in." I can still recall the exact sound of her little-girl voice as she balked at the door to the recital hall. It was an intimidating auditorium, filled with echoes. On the stage, the Steinway crouched like a slumbering black dragon.

"Okay," Dan said, immediately agreeable. "Let's go home." He had come under duress to begin with and was already chafing in his good shoes and starched shirt. He reached up to adjust the bill of the baseball cap that wasn't there. "Better yet, let's go for ice cream."

"We can't leave," I said, shooting daggers at him with my eyes. "Look, Moll, your name's already on the program." I showed her the printed sheet the piano teacher's son had given us at the door.

She refused to let go of Dan's hand. He was her ally and

suddenly I was the enemy. We stood on either side of her, locked in a silent tug-of-war.

Not for the first time, it occurs to me that he was always quick to back off while I played the ogre, pushing her into new situations, sometimes against her will. I wonder if I'm doing that now, pushing her across the country to college. Dan, like Travis, would prefer for her to go to the state school.

Elsewhere on the quilt is a rosette of red stretchy fabric from the swimsuit she wore when I delivered her to her first swim lesson. At the YMCA pool, she had clung to me like a remora. Her howl of panic ricocheted around the pool deck, and her slippery, strong little body strained toward the locker room. Dan had rescued her that day, coming out on deck in his board shorts, looking like a hunk on *Baywatch* as he snatched her up. I was furious with him, but didn't want to make even more of a scene, so I bit my tongue. He took her by the hand and led her away from the noisy echo chamber of shrieks, punctuated by coaches' whistles.

An hour later, I found them both in the rec pool. "Watch me, Mommy, watch!" Molly yelled, and leaped off the side, disappearing under the surface. She sprang up and swam, struggling like a puppy, straight to her waiting father. "See?" she said, her wide eyes starred by wet lashes, "I don't need lessons."

This is different, I thought at the recital. He can't save her from the piano. He can only help her run away.

In the end, the decision was taken from all of us. "There you are," said Mrs. Dashwood, the piano teacher, bustling forward. "Let's go backstage and get some lipstick on." The teacher, who had an MFA and the face of a pageant winner, was idolized by her little-girl students. Mrs. Dashwood was wise, too, understanding the power of the promise of stage makeup to distract a kid from fear. She took Molly by the hand and walked her down the sloping aisle of the auditorium.

Molly glanced back once, her eyes filled with uncertainty, yet she was unresisting as Mrs. Dashwood led her away. I watched the teacher stop at the edge of the stage to point something out. By the time Molly disappeared behind the curtain, there was a discernible spring of excitement in her step.

I found myself clutching Dan's hand. I didn't even remember grabbing it, but I would never forget what he said. Leaning down to kiss my cheek, he said, "Relax. She's in good hands."

"Hey, if it were up to you, she'd be at the ice-cream parlor."

"And guess what—the world wouldn't come to an end."

As the youngest on the program, Molly went first. Mrs. Dashwood welcomed everyone, then introduced her. A smattering of applause and a few adoring "Awws" came from the audience, which consisted of carefully dressed parents, grandparents and the occasional doting aunt or restless sibling.

Molly walked slowly with a curious dignity, her full skirt tolling like a bell with each step she took. So tiny, I thought. A porcelain doll, all alone up there. She didn't look at the audience, didn't try to find me with her eyes. She stood still, and my heart skipped a beat. But Molly knew what she was doing. She jacked up the stool to its highest level so she could reach the keyboard.

We had practiced how to smooth the full skirt in order to sit down properly. She remembered every unhurried move. Her patent leather shoes glittered in the stage lights, dangling above the pedals. Mrs. Dashwood said she wouldn't use the pedals until she was tall enough to reach them.

She rested her little hands on the keyboard. This was it, I thought. This was her moment. I took in a breath, ready to be dazzled.

It was a disaster from the first chord. Wrong notes, hesitation, whole measures forgotten. It was the longest ninety seconds of my life.

When it was over, I had aged a decade. Molly barely made it through the adorable curtsy we'd rehearsed. She fled into the wings and we found her in the stage hallway, a crushed flower surrounded by blue petals.

"This is the worst thing that ever happened to me," she sobbed, going limp against Dan when he picked her up. "This is worse than missing *larynx* in the spelling bee."

"I still can't spell *larynx*," I murmured.

"We should have gone for ice cream," Dan said.

In the passenger seat of the Suburban, I dart my needle into the heart of the fabric, quilting it with the words, "Be audacious." The cornflower-blue fabric is like new. Molly never wore the dress again.

She didn't give up piano, though. Following the recital, she walked into the house, went straight to the piano and played the Bach flawlessly, every note ringing sweet and true through the empty rooms. "Just to make sure I could," she said.

Glancing over from the driver's seat now, Molly notices me working the blue piece. "What's that one?" she asked.

I angle it toward her. "Your first piano recital."

"I don't remember that dress."

"Bach's 'Minuet in G Major.'" The name of the piece usually jogged her memory.

"I'm blanking. Cute fabric, though."

Funny how the heart holds its memories, or lets them go. Each detail of that day is etched into me. I can even remember the flavor of ice cream we got afterward—maple walnut with chocolate sprinkles. Yet Molly has cast the nerves and trauma of that day from her mind. They are not important to her.

"Remember that red silk charmeuse you wore to your senior adjudication last January?" I ask her.

"Of course. I brought it along to keep you from cutting it up," she says, her urgency making me smile. "I love that dress."

"I know. I figured you'd want to wear it again." Unlike the flounces and sashes of her childhood, the red dress makes her look truly grown-up, slender and elegant. Maybe even sexy, with its clinging shape and single bare shoulder. In the same auditorium where she'd once stumbled through a minuet, she had performed last on the program. Supple as a ribbon of scarlet silk in a breeze, she had swayed through a grand, emotional rendition of Chopin's "Nocturne in C Minor," a piece he composed when he was seventeen, the same age Molly was.

Mrs. Dashwood, scarcely changed from the no-nonsense teacher we'd known for years, had handed her a tube of

Chanel lipstick and declared her one of her most accomplished students ever.

The adjudicator gave Molly the highest possible marks and pronounced her the winner of the competition. Had she played better than the other students? It was hard to say. The adjudicator was Italian, a retired professor from the state college. All the other competitors were boys. It was hard not to miss the professor's enthusiasm for a pretty, talented girl in a red dress.

Still, I believed she had outdone the others in more than just looks. She had a gift. That nocturne sang with feeling. She knew how to take a heartfelt emotion and fling it wide for all to hear.

I'm kind of glad she doesn't remember the first disastrous recital. But I'm also glad I pushed her to do it. It occurs to me how much simpler it is to push your child in the right direction rather than yourself.

Molly flicks on the turn signal and drifts over to the right lane.

"What are you doing?" I ask.

"Thread, remember? You need thread."

The Suburban glides down the exit ramp and she takes a right, following a sign that points to "City Center."

Before too long, we find one of those chain craft and fabric stores. "They won't have the right kind," I lament.

"Then get another kind. No biggie." She catches the look on my face. "You should have brought more of the magical thread, if it's so important."

We step into the bright commercial glare of the craft shop. "You're right," I admit, "but Minerva's ran out and won't be getting in any more. She's closing the shop, you know."

"Nope, I didn't know. I thought it was for sale."

"It is. She's retiring and selling the place, but I doubt she'll find a buyer in this economy. I'll miss it. All her customers will. The idea of driving all the way to Rock Springs has no appeal to me at all."

"Bummer," Molly says, tucking her thumbs in her back pockets as she regards a display of notions.

As always, beautiful fabrics draw my eye. A few impossible-to-resist fat quarters make it into my shopping basket. The lure of a new project beckons. This happens a lot; I get close to the end of one thing and another pops into mind, seductive and infinitely more alluring than the project at hand.

At the end of a multitiered aisle, Molly fingers a green glass suncatcher marked Special of the Week. "Can I get this?"

My knee-jerk reaction is, *You don't need more junk*. But she takes after me, a magpie drawn to every glittering object that catches her eye. She's always been this way. Besides, it's in the shape of a music note, and it's only five bucks.

"One more pit stop," Molly says. Instead of going to the car, she heads into the shop across the way, a department store named Bradner's.

I happily follow her. It's fun shopping with someone who has her figure; everything looks good on her. But when I step into the store, I catch a whiff of White Shoulders perfume. This doesn't seem like Molly's kind of shop.

"What do you need, sweetie?"

"Come on," she says, her eyes sparkling. "We're going to pick out some new clothes for you."

"But…"

"But *what*, Mom?" Her excitement flashes to annoyance. The usual litany of excuses piles up: I don't need new clothes. I don't have time. I don't want to spend the money. I want to lose some weight before I buy a bunch of things. *I'm not important enough.*

I look at Molly and grin. "Let's do it."

She did not inherit her fashion smarts from me. Must be all those style blogs and glossy magazines she loves to read. When she teams up with a salesgirl named Darcy, there is no stopping the two of them. I surrender to their superior savvy and wait in a big double dressing room in a bra and panties that have seen better days, bare feet in need of a pedicure.

The glaring fluorescent lights and full-length, three-way mirror have no mercy. I stare at myself in triplicate, the images growing smaller and smaller into infinity. Molly and Darcy bring in tops, slacks and jeans, silky cardigans and jackets nipped in at the waist, belts and low-heeled pumps. They can't resist accessorizing with statement jewelry, bright scarves, slender hoop earrings. The attention feels good—and the clothes look good on me.

Molly hands me a cream leather hobo bag. "You are so pretty, Mom. Wait until Dad sees you. Wait until everyone sees you."

In the end, I buy about half of what she wants me to get. Even that seems excessive to me, but with all the nice things to choose from, it was hard to narrow them down. We walk out of the store with a parcel as big as the quilt bag. It's filled with new jeans and shoes, a top and sweater and skirt, a wrap dress and hoop earrings, and a melon-colored paisley scarf I couldn't bear to leave behind. Molly and Darcy made me keep the new undergarments on, leaving my elastic-less ones in the trash. "When you start with a good foundation," Darcy pointed out, "everything looks better."

"Well," I say, setting the shopping bag on the backseat next to the quilt. "That was unexpected."

"That was fun," Molly said. "Way more fun than a fabric shop."

"A different kind of fun than the fabric shop."

She's not done, and her enthusiasm is infectious. On Darcy's recommendation, we go to a nearby salon for a shampoo and style. We have our toenails polished candy pink and emerge from the salon flipping our hair around and giggling.

"Look at us," Molly says, primping in the Suburban's visor mirror. "We're new women."

Chapter Eight

The next day, the sheen is off our hair. Molly urges me to wear something new but I decline, not wanting to wrinkle the clothes, sitting in the car all day. The bag with the beautiful new things stays on the backseat. The outfits are too nice for a car trip. I want to save them for something special.

According to the peeling roadside billboards, we have two choices for lunch—a Stuckey's that has ninety-nine-cent burgers, or Bubba's Beach Shack, on the scenic shores of Lake Ontario.

"It's a lake," Molly says. "How can it have a beach?"

"It's one of the Great Lakes." I am nearly cross-eyed from sewing. The end of our journey looms closer, an outcome I can see and practically touch. I stayed up late last night, working on the quilt. Working is, of course, an elastic concept. I can be staring out at the night sky and call it "working" if I'm planning the next quilt.

"I never thought about a lake having a beach. Back home it's just…a shore, I guess."

"We should have taken you to see the Great Lakes when you were little." And here it is again, that sense of things left undone, unfinished. What else have I forgotten to show her, to teach her?

She glances over at me. "You took me to Mount Rushmore and Yosemite and the Grand Canyon and the Everglades. You can't show me everything."

"I wish I had, though. We always had such fun on those summer driving trips, didn't we?"

There is a heartbeat of hesitation. And in that heartbeat, I hear a contradiction. Could be, she has memories of being hot, carsick, bored. Sometimes Dan and I were short-tempered and we were terrible at picking out places to stay. Bad motel karma became a family joke. Remembrances of summers past are marred by nonfunctioning swimming pools, moldy smells, shag carpets.

"Sure," Molly says. "We had a blast."

"But the Great Lakes—I remember going to Mackinac Island on my high school senior trip. I saved up for months in order to go. It was so beautiful, like stepping back in time. I wish we'd taken you there."

"You can't take me everywhere," she repeats.

New adventures lie ahead of her, a vast stretch of unexplored terrain. She'll be taking trips without me, seeing and experiencing things I'll never share. Which is as it should be, I remind myself.

Without further debate, she takes the next exit and wends her way through a threadbare town of redbrick buildings and convenience stores plastered with fading advertising posters. The route to Bubba's is well-marked, and within a few minutes we enter Tanaka State Park in western New York, a quiet oasis on a weekday afternoon. As we head toward the water, I notice that the colors of summer are fading here, the greens subtly shifting to yellow, the wild-flowers casting their petals to the breeze.

The beach shack is adorable, and I'm instantly glad we've come. It has a huge deck with picnic tables covered in red-and-white checkered oilcloth, and a long dock reaching out to the deep, wind-crested waters of the lake. And it truly is a beach, fringed by sand and weathered by wave action. From this perspective, the lake looks as infinite as the sea itself. There are even herring gulls here, and I wonder if they lost their way and became landlocked, and if that would matter to a bird.

The waiter is the sort of gorgeous teenage boy who makes me feel like an urban cougar as I check him out. I can check him out as much as I want, because he has not even noticed me. He's eyeing Molly. Who wouldn't? Boys have always been drawn in by her pretty eyes, her smile that hints that she knows a secret.

We order the fish fry lunch, and it arrives in paper-lined baskets with French fries and coleslaw. It's beautiful here, and graceful boats skim across the water in the distance, the sails puffed out in the breeze.

"Check that out," Molly says, indicating a parasail kite flying from the back of a speedboat.

"Yikes, looks scary."

"Looks awesome." She dips a French fry in her coleslaw, a habit she acquired from Dan ages ago. She gazes dreamily at the sky, studying the little sailing man with stick legs, like a paratrooper GI Joe.

As we watch, the parasail is reeled into the back of the boat, and they tie up at the dock right below the restaurant.

"It's definitely awesome," the cute waiter says, coming to refill our iced-tea glasses. From the pocket of his half apron, he hands her a card. "Here's a coupon for $5 off a ride."

I shake my head. "We won't be needing—"

"Thanks." Molly snatches the card. "Thanks a lot."

"We're not doing it." I dole out cash to cover our tab, leaving a generous tip even though I wish he hadn't put ideas in Molly's head.

"Come on, Mom. We've got time." Ignoring my protests, she heads down the stairs to the dock, her steps light with excitement. When I get to her side, she's already talking with the guys in the speedboat.

"It takes fifteen minutes," she says, "and we won't even get wet, except maybe our feet."

"We're not doing it."

"Ma'am, it's very safe. I've been doing this for years," the boat driver assures me.

I hate looking like a stick-in-the-mud. But I also hate the idea of dangling several hundred feet above the lake, tethered to the world by a rope no bigger than my finger.

Molly has that expression on her face. I don't see it often, but when I do, I know she means business. The stubborn jaw, the fire in her eye. A minute later, she's signing a faded pink form on a clipboard without reading it, and asking if I'll pay the fee. I haven't read the disclaimer, either, but I'm sure it absolves the boat guys of any liability if we happen to wind up at the bottom of Lake Ontario.

Studying the form over her shoulder, I point out one line. "It says here you need to weigh at least a hundred pounds. Last I knew, you were just under that."

She shrugs it off. "After this summer, I'm well over a hundred."

The boat guys seem to believe her. They put her in a high-tech life vest and helmet and she kicks off her shoes.

"A helmet?" I ask.

"Just a safety precaution," the man says.

I want to ask how a helmet is going to keep her safe if she plummets into the lake. I want to say that she's never tipped the scale past a hundred pounds, but I stop myself. It's my nature to cite the potential disaster in every situation. I recognize that. So, apparently, does Molly, because she learned to dismiss my fears years ago. She has gone mountain biking, horseback riding, scuba diving. A spirit of adventure is good, I remind myself. It's small and mean of me to dampen it.

Just the other day, I was thinking about what a pushy mother I've been. But the things I pushed her to do didn't place life and limb at risk. Especially pointless risk.

She's grinning ear-to-ear as they harness her to the sail. "'Bye, Mom," she says. "See you when I come back around."

"Be careful," I can't help saying, and now there's a fire in *my* eye as I send out warning signals to the boat driver and his helper.

Then there is nothing more to say as they head away from the dock, the big engine cutting a V-shaped wake behind the boat. My heart is in my throat as they reach open water, and the rainbow-colored sail fills with wind.

Then, a moment later, Molly is aloft, a tiny doll tethered by a slender cord. She flies like a kite tail, higher and higher until they run out of rope. I shade my eyes and look at her, silhouetted by the sun.

Then my heart settles and I wave both arms wildly over my head. "Go, Molly!" I shout, jumping up and down on the dock. "Go, Molly!"

Watching her fly is incredibly gratifying. I fumble with my mobile phone, try to get a picture to send to Dan. She'll probably look like no more than a speck against the sky, but he'll get the idea.

A gust of wind ripples across the water in a discernible path. I can actually see the gust filling the sail and then turning it sideways. Molly's stick-figure legs swing to and fro like a pendulum.

"Omigod," I say. "Omigod, she's going to fall."

Apparently the boat driver knows something isn't right. His partner starts cranking in the cord, his movements fast, maybe frantic. I stand motionless on the dock, my feet riveted to the planks, my stomach a ball of ice. Here is the definition of hell—knowing something terrible is happening to your child and being completely powerless to stop it.

If she dies, I think with grim clarity, so will I.

The wind whips her like a rag doll. Her screams sound faint. I wonder if she's calling my name. I send up a prayer, pushing it out with every cell of my body and soul.

The screams grow louder, and then I realize she's not screaming at all. She's laughing.

Chapter Nine

"You should try it," Molly says, combing back her wind-tossed hair and pulling it into a bun. She is still shivering from the lake, her lips tinged a subtle blue. With her hair pulled back, she looks sophisticated, older. We return to the beach shack to get her something warm to drink. The hunky waiter hovers, bringing her hot tea in a small stainless steel pot.

"In my next life, maybe."

"Seriously, Mom, you'd love it."

"I'm too chicken to love something like that." Still, I feel a slight twinge. What would it be like, dangling in midair like the tail of a giant kite? But no. That is so far out of my comfort zone I can't even imagine myself doing it.

"What's that piece of fabric?" Molly asks, indicating the dotted Swiss. She's been enjoying my stories about the pieces in the quilt.

"This is from your grandmother's square-dancing skirt.

There's plenty of fabric, yards and yards of it, so I used it for sashing. Do you remember how she and Grandpa used to go square dancing?"

"Sort of. Maybe just from looking at old pictures, though."

My parents were avid square dancers. They belonged to a club that held a dance the first Saturday of every month. I can still see them in my mind's eye, my dad trim and dapper in a Western-cut shirt, with mother-of-pearl snap buttons, and a string tie. My mother's dresses were outrageous confections. She made them herself, with yards of ruched calico or dotted Swiss draped over a pinwheel froth of crinolines. The dresses had puffy sleeves that sat like weightless balls on her shoulders, and she always wore these horrible little one-strap dancing shoes.

The sight of my folks in their square-dancing getup might have made me squirm, except that they were so damn happy to be going out to the dance hall together, to laugh with their friends and drink sticky fruit punch.

"They loved those dances so much," I tell Molly, drawing a stitch through the sashing. "Grandma more than Grandpa, but he was a good sport about it."

"I never saw them dance," Molly says.

"Every once in a while, they'd have family night and we'd go." Of course she wouldn't remember that; she was in a stroller at the time. Still, I could see her swinging her tiny feet and clapping, mesmerized by the noise and the movements.

When Molly was in the second grade, my mother suffered a massive stroke. She was just sixty-four; it shouldn't have happened. I took Molly to see her, praying my child wouldn't act frightened when she saw Mom's altered face, the left side slack and unresponsive, her neck encased in a cervical collar.

I needn't have worried. Molly had happily rolled an ergonomic table in front of my mother and said, "Now you can play cards with me."

The funny, sewing, square-dancing mom I knew vanished that day, even though she lived for two more years. Her personality changed, and dark anger emerged from a place we never knew was inside her. It was as if the stroke awakened a slumbering dragon inside her. She raged at how hard she had worked, and how frustrated she was that she hadn't given her kids more. I constantly reassured her that what she'd given her family was enough. She always liked it when I brought Molly to visit her, though. Seeing her only granddaughter quieted the angry sadness.

She was supposed to get better with a long and rigorous course of physical and occupational therapy. She hated the therapy, though—squeezing a hard blue rubber ball, poking a thick shoelace through holes on a board to form the shape of a spider, walking back and forth between parallel bars. Most days, she refused to do any of it, preferring to let my dad tie her shoes and push her wheelchair. Her hands, which used to effortlessly knit Fair Isle sweaters and mittens and hats, closed around some invisible object and refused to open. Once or twice, she tried knitting again, but the yarn wound up in knots of frustration on the floor. The physical therapists told my father that in the long run, she'd be better off dressing herself and learning to walk on her own, but Dad didn't listen. It was more important to him to do what my mom wanted.

"I wish I could remember the square dancing," Molly says. "Not the assisted-living place."

I wish that, too. Even though I know it's irrational, I feel irritated at Molly because she doesn't remember my mother the way I want her to. I want her to recall the funny singing voice, the strong hands with their faint smell of onion, the perfect bulb of hair held slick with Aqua-Net. I want Molly to miss *that* woman, even though I understand it's impossible.

"How did she die?" Molly asks. "You never talk about that."

"Ask me how she lived. After all, that's what she spent most of her life doing."

"You talk about that all the time," Molly notes. "And I do love hearing the stories, Mom. But you've made her into this Disney grandma who's barely real to me."

"She got pneumonia and was too weak to fight it." I smooth my hand over the fading calico. "She died early one morning when you were in fourth grade. I didn't tell you right away because you had a school party that day. I didn't want to ruin it for you. So I waited until you got home."

Molly is quiet for a minute, sipping her tea, staring out across the lake, where the wind whips up white tufts in the water. Wrapped in a blanket someone at the restaurant gave her, she looks little and lost. But there is a sharpness in her eyes. "You were always cushioning me, Mom."

"It's what mothers do." I wish my own mother could see this young woman now, vibrant and excited about her future. My dad, who has grown quiet and slow with age and loneliness, often tells me he wishes that, too.

"It didn't work," she says, not looking at me. "I knew,

anyway. I could tell from the way you rushed me off to carpool. I was scared to say anything because I didn't want to see you cry."

This shocks me. Dan and I had been prepared; Mom's doctors had let us know her death was imminent, even offering signs and markers to watch for. For me, the sense of loss was so overwhelming that I hadn't been able to talk about it.

Even now, years later, it's still hard. There is something about losing your mother that is permanent and inexpressible—a wound that will never quite heal.

"I had a rotten day at school that day," Molly explains. "Hated the party. There were these awful cupcakes, and the games were lame. So it's not like you spared me anything."

"Moll, I never realized you knew what was going on that day."

"Nope. You didn't. I didn't say anything because I didn't want to upset you. We were both trying to protect each other, and it didn't work."

I draw the thread to the end and make a tiny, invisible knot before cutting it free. "How did you get so smart?"

"Must've inherited it from my mother. We'd better get going." She drinks the last of her tea, combs her hair again. The breeze is reviving her curls. She stands up and folds the blanket. She waves a thank-you to the waiter and he hurries over to our table.

I put my things into the crafter's bag and head back to the car while she lingers to talk to the waiter. Looking back, I feel a jab of annoyance. I don't like the way he stands so close to her, checking her out. It's on the tip of my tongue to call out, to remind them both that I'm standing here.

Then I think about what Molly said about me always stepping in, trying to smooth things over for her, to absorb the body blows life tends to deal out from time to time.

The afternoon at the lake caused an almost imperceptible shift in our mood. We're more on edge. Our silences are longer, corresponding to the flat, boring stretches of highway.

How do long-haul truck drivers handle the tedium? How will I handle it, driving back alone, the Suburban emptied of Molly's things, devoid of her fruity-smelling hair products and her lively chatter?

What's really eating me is this. We're almost there.

Odometer Reading 123,597

"No other border was applied with
greater ingenuity and diversity
than the Sawtooth. It could be applied
in one of three methods to a perfect
turn and direction, but it is in its less
precise applications that it often assumed
its greatest charm."

—Sandi Fox,
Small Endearments, 19th Century Quilts for Children

Chapter Ten

There is a change in Molly's phone calls with Travis. Pacing back and forth, the tiny silver phone glued to her ear, she talks to him at every rest stop, it seems. The shift in tone and emphasis is subtle but palpable. She is both more animated and more intense.

I don't say anything, of course. What is there to say? They're eighteen, and in love.

Give it time, I remind myself. The drifting-apart is not going to happen overnight. I picture the two of them like the huge layers of ice we get on the lake back home. All winter long, the frozen surface is strong and impermeable; the skating goes on for weeks. Yet in spring, the ice cracks apart, and once that happens, the pieces never fit together properly again. Even if the temperature drops sufficiently at night to re-freeze the ice, it's not the same; it's rough and chunky, prone to breaking. The skaters all go home for the season.

Separation is rough on any relationship. On a pair who have barely dipped a toe into adulthood, it's usually a death knell. They just don't have the emotional hardware to sustain a love that depends on physical closeness. And I won't kid myself. Those two were close. They were physical.

I can't imagine Travis Spellman going dateless for movie nights or football games, not for long. Likewise, I don't want Molly to be like a war widow at college, holding back from the social scene because of her hometown boyfriend.

That lack of availability, physical and emotional, is undoubtedly what will cause them to go their separate ways, as they must. Molly has a future ahead of her filled with brand-new people, challenging studies, a city she's never seen before. Settling into college will take all her time and energy. Nurturing a long-distance relationship is simply not feasible.

Except, of course, that she believes it is. And here's the thing about my daughter. If she believes in something with her whole heart, no one can tell her otherwise.

At a rest stop where we park to stretch our legs and use the facilities, she is pacing back and forth on the sere, dun-colored grass that has gone dormant from drought. The phone is still glued to her ear and her flip-flops kick up dust in her wake.

I wander along the walkway of the rest stop. It's a pleasant spot, insulated from the noise of the interstate by a stand of thick trees, evergreens and sugar maples that are just getting ready to take on their fall colors.

The local historical society in this area has a craft booth set up at the rest stop, and I buy a bottle of amber maple syrup from a woman in a homespun apron and—I kid you not—a poke bonnet. The clear glass bottle is in the shape of a maple leaf, and when I hold it up to the sun, it sparkles like a jewel.

According to the information flyer that came with the syrup, the maple trees will put on a dazzling display of fall color. These country roads will soon be crowded with RVs and busloads of leaf-lookers, coming to enjoy the scenery so beautiful that it attracts tourists from the world over to view them each year. After the riot of color, the trees lose all their leaves and appear to die.

Yet it is then, in the dead of winter, that the maples are most productive. If you tap deep enough into the tree, sinking a metal tube into its most hidden heart, you'll discover a gush of life.

The sap is drained through the tube, collected in covered buckets and boiled in huge vats to make maple syrup.

Who the heck thought of that? I wonder. At some moment in the unremembered past, someone walked up to a leafless maple tree, hammered a tube into its center, harvested the sap and rendered it into sweet syrup. What a random thing to do.

One thing I'd guess—whoever thought it up wasn't a college graduate. She—I'm quite certain it was a *she*—was probably a mother. An ancient Algonquin desperate housewife. At the end of a long winter, her kids were probably bored and cranky from being cooped up in the longhouse, chasing each other and driving her crazy with their noise. They had no idea supplies had run low, that the men hadn't done too well on the latest hunt. Pretty soon, the kids' war whoops and giggles would turn to whining. Yelling at the older kids to keep the younger ones away from the fire, the woman strapped on snowshoes made of hide, with gut laces, and trudged out into the deadening cold to look for food.

How did she know about the secret inside the maple tree? Maybe the deer clued her in. During the starving season, the hungry animals stripped the bark from the trees as high as they could reach. Maybe the woman, her vision sharpened by desperation, noticed the glistening ooze from the flesh of the trees. Maybe she touched a finger to the sticky dampness, tasted a faint sweetness on her tongue. And the rest was history. An industry was born. The hunting party came home with their limp, skinny rabbit to find the women and children feasting on boiled cornmeal, magically sweetened with an elixir from the sugar maples.

I reach the end of the walkway and wander back. The woman in the poke bonnet is standing behind her booth, furtively smoking a cigarette.

Still on the phone, Molly notices me watching her and wanders over to an information board covered with maps and tourist brochures. She tucks one hand into the back pocket of her shorts and keeps talking.

Her face is bright with love.

Seeing her like this conjures up mixed emotions. On the one hand, I am proud and gratified that my daughter has a great heart, that she can give it away with joy and sincerity. Yet on the other, I wish she understood the difference between the passionate heat of first love and the deep security of a lasting commitment.

But there is no difference, not in Molly's mind, and no amount of discussion—lecturing, she would call it—on my part will change her mind about that. Love is love, she'd tell me, and who am I to say she's wrong? I can't claim to be an expert. There is a part of me—and it's not even a small part—that keeps wondering what my marriage will be like when I get home and it's just Dan and me.

Agitated, I take a seat at an empty picnic table, which faces a lovely marsh fringed by cattails, the reeds clacking in the light breeze. The distant hiss of truck brakes joins the singing of frogs from the marsh.

I pull out the quilt, thinking I'll add a stitch or two. The feel of the age-softened fabrics is oddly soothing. Yet at the same time, I am nagged by the sense that I wish I'd never started this thing. What a crazy notion, to think I could actually put the final touches in place in time for the journey's end.

"That's a beautiful piece," someone says, and I look up to see a woman about my age, walking a scruffy little dog on a retractable leash. The dog ranges out to the end of the leash and then comes reeling back toward her, like a yo-yo on a string. The woman is checking out the quilt with a practiced eye.

"Thanks," I say, recognizing the expertise with which she studies the project. It's gratifying to realize quilters are everywhere. It's such a universal art, beloved by so many women. "I'm making this for my daughter's dorm room."

She nods appreciatively. "What a great idea. Wow, are you hand quilting?"

"More portable that way. More variety." This morning I stitched the word *Remember* across a piece made from my mom's square-dancing dress.

"I've always thought crazy quilting was much more challenging than a regular pattern," the stranger remarks.

"You might be right. At first, I thought it would make

the work to go faster. Instead, I keep trying to force things together and changing my mind."

"I like going slowly when I quilt," she comments. "It keeps me in the moment, you know?"

I do know. And here's what happens when quilting women meet. When one quilter encounters another, there's always something to talk about. We go from being strangers to friends in about three seconds. I've seen this happen again and again, back home at the shop. It's like the fabric itself is common ground, the pattern a secret handshake. Quilting women already know so much about each other. We get to skip over the petty details.

Within moments, I am giving her a guided tour of Molly's quilt—the snippet of fabric from the tooth fairy pillow, upon which she placed her first lost tooth. The blue ribbon she won at the seventh-grade science fair, for her pond-water display. A Girl Scout badge she earned delivering Christmas cookies to a nursing home. One square is decorated with pink loops of ribbon in honor of the time she raised a thousand dollars in a Race for the Cure.

Sometimes I wonder if I'm being fair with the milestones and memories I'm stitching into this quilt. It's easy to block out a square to celebrate her little victories and happy times. But what about a square to commemorate her detention notes for skipping school, or the time she pierced her own navel and it got infected, or the night the local police brought her home, reeking of peach-flavored wine cooler? Why not remember those times? They're part of her history, too.

"You're making a family heirloom," the woman remarks.

Ha, I think, vindicated. That's why I don't need those

reminders in the quilt. "It's not going to be finished in time."

The woman smiles, leans back against the picnic table. "In time for what?"

"Move-in day at the dorm."

"I have a rule. If it's not falling apart, it's finished." She is about my age, I surmise, yet she seems wiser, and I'm not sure why. Her posture is relaxed, and she appears to be in no hurry.

I tell her about the shop back home, how I'll miss it when it's gone, how it won't be the same, buying my fabric somewhere else.

"Maybe someone will take over," the woman suggests.

"I sure hope so. I'm not optimistic, though. Most of the women I know who'd be capable already have other jobs, or they're retired, or too busy with their families. It's a huge risk and a huge commitment."

"I hear you," the woman says. The dog has finished its business in the reeds, and she calls out to a little girl who is playing on the swing set. "Amanda, we'd better get going."

The dark-haired child runs over on chubby legs. "Five more minutes," she begs in a voice every woman within earshot recognizes.

"One more," my companion says, and we both know it will stretch out to five.

"Your daughter's adorable," I tell her.

"Thanks, but she's not my daughter." The woman glances over at Molly, her fleeting look filled with insight. "Amanda's my granddaughter."

Oh, man. She's a grandmother. I don't want to be a grandmother. I'm not finished being a mother.

Yet when she finally reels in her dog and calls to the dark-haired little girl, and Amanda runs into her arms, there is a magical joy in their bond. It's sweeter, somehow, than motherhood, probably because it's simpler.

"Drive safely," I tell them.

"You do the same," she says, "and good luck with the quilt."

Chapter Eleven

On the final leg of our journey, the landscape is a patchwork of forest, field, stream and village, stitched together at the seams by country roads and rock or whitewashed fences.

"God, do people actually live here?" Molly wonders aloud, taking it slow as she navigates the Suburban down a hill to an old-fashioned town, complete with white church spire and village green. "It looks like a movie set."

She's right. It's a strange and beautiful land, innocent and pristine, yet with a faint air of danger that comes with alien territory. As a girl, I dreamed of traveling far, but I never did. In my family, vacations were few and far between, and when we went somewhere, it was usually a car trip to a state park. For my parents, life at home was enough.

My mother had a favorite escape, and it was as simple as turning on the TV. She was fanatical about the TV soap *Dallas,* about a family like none we'd ever known. In my head, I hear the brassy theme song that heralded the start of the show. It's one of the most vivid memories of my childhood. The churning melody signaled my dad's bowling night and my mother's sacrosanct program. On Sunday nights, the routine never varied. She would shoo him out the door, then fix an Appian Way pizza out of the box, oiling her hands with Wesson and expertly spreading the dough in a thin circle on a round baking sheet. A splash of canned tomato sauce, a sprinkle of questionable-looking cheese, and heaven was only minutes away.

Unlike any other day of the week, we didn't have a proper, sit-down family dinner on Sundays. No salad or side dishes, no pretense of a token vegetable. Just slices of hot pizza and glasses of cold milk. Maybe a Little Debbie for dessert.

Then, despite my deeply resentful protests and martyrlike sighs, I was sent to bed. Even in the summer, when the light lingered for an extra hour, Mom made me decamp upstairs to my room, because Sunday nights were sacred. They were *Dallas* nights.

Mom wanted no interruptions. I suppose she would have taken the phone off the hook, but she didn't have to, because all her friends were doing the same thing—hastening their children off to bed, urging their husbands out the door—so they could spend an hour in that fabled living-color world of millionaire matrons and the scoundrels who loved them.

I wasn't allowed to watch and wouldn't have wanted to, anyway. To a kid, the endless adult conversations, high-stakes oil deals and secret affairs were deadly.

Sequestered in my room, I always knew when the show started. First, there would be the clink of a glass. On Sunday nights, Mom opened the wicker-clad bottle of jug wine we kept in the cupboard and poured herself exactly one round-bellied, stemmed glass, full to the brim. Next, a curl of cigarette smoke would snake its way upstairs, emanating from a Parliament 100 with recessed filter, whatever that meant. It was all part of Mom's curious ritual of self-indulgence. I wonder if she ever imagined Southfork Ranch as a real place, tucked into the green folds of the Texas countryside, with skyscrapers in the distance.

The high-octane music would swell, the sound boiling up the stairs to my resentful ears. Mom loved the theme from that show so much that she bought the sheet music. Even though we didn't have a piano, she learned to hum the notes. A few years ago, Molly found the music in the piano bench and picked it out while I was working in the kitchen. I felt the same curious shiver of resentment and intrigue I'd felt as a child.

Nowadays, women escape by running away to urban spas, yoga retreats or wild-woman weekends of paintball drills and primal screams. Others frequent male strip clubs or dress to the nines for high tea. Back then, women like my mom didn't have to go any farther than their living rooms.

We stop at a deli for a take-away lunch, and Molly is drawn to the counter girl's flat New England accent, which skips blithely over the "r" and elongates the vowels.

The sub sandwiches are called "grinders," and the milk-shakes are "frappes." The word feels awkward and foreign in my mouth, and when we place our order, Molly and I don't look at each other because we'll start giggling.

We take our lunch to a roadside park with a scenic overlook. There is a sign pointing the way to the Norman Rockwell home.

"I can see where he got his inspiration," I tell Molly, gesturing at the spill of rounded mountains below us.

"Who?"

"Norman Rockwell." I indicate the signpost.

"Who's that?"

Not again. This is crazy. Is it possible that she isn't familiar with the quintessential American artist of the twentieth century?

"You know, the one who did all the illustrations of kids fishing and families praying," I say. "He did the cover of the *Saturday Evening Post* for years. That was even before my time, but you saw those illustrations everywhere—calendars, greeting cards, posters, dentist's offices."

"I guess."

"Maybe we could drive over there, check out the place where he created his art."

"Let's not." She speaks quickly. Maybe there's an edge of urgency in her voice.

I let the topic go. "I've got one thing to say about grinders and frappes, or frapp-ays, however you say it."

"What's that?"

"They rock."

She nods in agreement. The homemade bread and exotic cold cuts—olive loaf, dry salami, maple-smoked ham—and tart dressing and relish are delicious. I tell myself I can start my diet when I get home.

It's too nice a day to hurry. Molly decides to take a walk, her euphemism for going somewhere private in order to call Travis. I doubt she'll get a cell phone signal here, but I don't say anything. Instead, I pull out the quilt and jab my needle into the fabric, piercing through all the layers. The quick silver flash travels fast, but not fast enough. Bit by bit, I am coming to realize that I have failed. By the time we get to the college, the quilt still won't be finished.

Feeling unsettled, I watch Molly walking down the road, hands in her back pockets. Suddenly she looks very small and alone to me, and the urge to protect her—from what? Who knows?—rises up strong in me. Soon I won't be around to protect her. But she has to go.

And as for me, I have to let her. After that, I have to figure out how to be my own person again.

"What's that look?" Molly asks, returning from her walk and sitting beside me at the picnic table.

"I don't have a look."

"Come on. Spill."

"Just thinking of this huge change. It feels so sudden."

"It's not like we didn't see it coming."

"I know. And this is what I wanted. I wanted to raise a child. And I did, I raised a wonderful child. But now you're leaving."

"Mom." She offers a sweet, ironic smile. "That's the whole point."

"Well, I just wish someone had told me how hard it is to let go."

"Did you think it would be easy?"

"Of course not." The needle darts again, in and out of the quilt.

"A little bird once told me you shouldn't avoid doing something just because it's hard."

My exact words, only I'd probably said them to her in order to get her to go off the diving board or eat a portobello mushroom.

"If you go away and screw up," I blurt out, "how will I help you fix it?" I am instantly horrified. What a stupid thing to say. An apology rushes up through me. It came out all wrong. I shouldn't have said that.

Before I can babble out *I'm sorry, I didn't mean it*, Molly bursts out laughing. "News flash, Mom. It's not your job to fix it."

I laugh with her, but I can't help the next thought that pops into my head: Then what *is* my job?

We spend longer than we intended at the roadside park. It's so pretty and the air feels so good. When the breeze shifts just so, I can sense the forward march of the season, and I can see it in the crowns of the distant trees in the high elevations, which are starting to turn.

Molly seems preoccupied. I wonder if she's thinking about what lies ahead—or what she left behind. Her phone calls and text messaging with Travis have decreased in frequency, which I take to be a good sign. She is driving while I keep doggedly working on the quilt, and she is fixated on the posted distance to the city. "Only forty more miles," she says. "Hard to believe we're finally that close."

My needle slides through the fabric, paying homage to a swatch of old flannel from Dan's pajamas, something she probably doesn't even remember. But I do and suddenly I miss the feel of his arms around me, the sound of his breathing, calm and steady. I think about his warmth and his scent as he sleeps beside me. I miss him. If he were here, he'd make me say exactly what's on my mind. No use bottling it up.

"I suppose we could go all the way right now," I say, "instead of finding a place to stay way out in the suburbs." We had planned for a noon arrival on orientation day, so she would have time to organize her dorm room before heading into the maze of new student activities.

"No." Her reply is surprisingly swift and firm. "That's not the plan. We don't want to get to the city after dark. And I bet there won't be any vacancies near the school, anyway, and even if we found a place to stay, the hotels are massively overpriced and the residence halls don't open to new students until tomorrow at noon."

Her barrage of protests is a bit mystifying. She couldn't wait to get to college but now, the night before her new life is set to begin, she seems to have all the time in the world. I'm gratified that she wants to extend our time together.

"You're right," I agree, and I watch out the window for the exit sign to the town we'd picked out as our final stop. "We should stick to the plan."

She nods and glances at her cell phone, lying on the seat beside her. Travis hasn't called all day, which I suspect is the cause of the prolonged silences that stretch between us. I, with a terrible and dark sense of satisfaction, find myself hoping this is the beginning of the end for them, that his failure to call is not due to the lack of a signal, but to the lack of commitment.

My own thoughts make me feel horrible. She adores Travis, and he makes her happy. Isn't that what I want for her, to be happy? Still, I don't want my daughter's future to belong to him, a charming local boy who has spent the entire summer trying to convince her that there is no better life than the one our small Western town has to offer.

It was enough for me, I realize with a surge of guilt, and I swiftly glance at her. There in that same small town she's been forced to leave, I've found all of life's happiness. Suppose I'm robbing her of the chance to do the same?

And why do I hope her dreams are bigger than mine ever were? What is it that I want for her that I never wanted for myself?

The onslaught of second thoughts assaults me. Molly flips on the turn signal. "This will do."

We have a club card for Travelers Rest, a chain of mid-range hotels, and so I nod in agreement. The room is predictable, clean and bland, a faint whiff of stale air blowing from the register vent. We are plenty early, with a large portion of the afternoon ahead of us. Maybe I'll finish Molly's quilt after all.

Instead, I am possessed by restlessness. I take the Suburban to a nearby station and fill it with gas, asking the attendant to check the oil, the tires, the wiper fluid. I use the squeegee to clear the squished bugs from the windshield and grill. It occurs to me that I performed this same routine the day I went into labor with Molly. In childbirth class, we'd been told that a woman on the brink of labor often experiences a burst of energy—the nesting instinct kicking in. I cleaned and scrubbed the house and car all day and was just settling down for a good night's sleep when my water broke.

So what is this, the de-nesting instinct? Simple common sense, I tell myself. Tomorrow, I don't want to be distracted by the menial tasks of checking gauges and tires. I want everything to go smoothly, with the Suburban as ready as a criminal's getaway car.

When I return to the motel, Molly is at the pool, a turquoise oval set in an apron of groomed grass. It's not exactly swimming weather, but this might be the last swim of the summer. So, despite the hint of a nip in the air, I decide to join her. I duck into the room, don my swimsuit, one of those figure-flattering jobs with hidden panels designed to suck everything in. Of course, it can't suck in what it doesn't cover, so I slip on the secret weapon of the forty-year-old woman—the cover-up.

My flip-flops slap against the sun-softened asphalt of the parking lot as I approach the pool. Molly is wearing the yellow-and-white bikini we picked out in the end-of-season sale at the mall back home, and her hair is slicked back, her skin dewy from swimming. She sits at the edge of the shallow end, watching two little kids, a boy and a girl who are maybe four and six.

I take in the sight of her, wondering when we'll travel together again, when we'll pick a motel because of its pool, when we'll eat junk food and watch TV together late into the night. Everything on this journey is more significant and intense because it's the last time.

The kids are laughing and splashing under the watchful eye of their mother, who turns occasionally to make conversation with Molly. As I watch, Molly wades in to help the little girl adjust her water wing, then holds her hand and turns her in a circle while making a motorboat sound. The little girl giggles and flails while I stand off to the side, watching. And suddenly I am seeing Molly and me, hearing our laughter echo across the water, feeling her tiny hand in mine as I lead the way.

I'm struck by how like me she is right now, angling her arm just so, making certain she's not going too fast or too deep for the small, trusting child. Where did she learn her gentleness with children, her humor? I don't remember teaching it, yet here she is, replicating a moment I didn't recall until just now. Suddenly, the memory is as clear to me as if it had happened the day before yesterday. One long-ago summer day, we looked exactly like this, a young woman and a little girl, sharing a small moment together.

Except I am not in the picture. This is Molly's moment, one that has nothing to do with me. And it's weirdly okay with me. She is her own person and I don't feel the need to insert myself into any of this.

Her cell phone, which is lying on a metal poolside table, suddenly goes off. Travis's ring sounds like a fire alarm.

Molly rushes to hand the little girl off to her mother, then leaps out of the pool, swift as a trained dolphin. She dabs her hand on a towel, then snatches up the phone. At the same moment, she sees me coming toward her.

Her face lights up with a glow of pure joy, a clear echo of the look she used to give me when she was tiny and I'd say, "Let's go for a swim, Moll."

She's lighting up for someone else now. She acknowledges me with a wave, then says into the phone, "Omigod. Omigod, really? I don't believe you!" She is jumping up and down now, a young adult no longer but a child bouncing with excitement. "Where?" she asks, and then, *"Now?"*

The settled feeling that had enveloped me only moments ago now swirls away. I set my towel on the chaise next to Molly's, wondering what's got her so excited. Here I thought she was uncoupling herself from Travis, their calls growing fewer and shorter as our journey progressed. Now she is as excited as she was when he asked her to prom.

Watching her, listening to the sparkle in her voice, I realize that I miss this Molly. Throughout this journey, she has been pleasant but guarded. Even soaring over Lake Ontario or watching line dancers at a honky tonk, she has been entertained, but not exuberant. Not until now.

What's he saying to her that causes the air to slip under her feet and lift her up?

And then with a laugh of joy, she drops the phone onto the table. "I don't believe it," she keeps saying and then she scoops up her flip-flops and runs. I am slow, not really hooked into this reality, not really believing it, either.

In slow motion I stand up and walk to the chainlink safety fence that surrounds the pool. Her bikini flashing in the sunlight, Molly races across the parking lot, shooting straight up in the air when the asphalt burns her feet, then hopping up and down as she throws her flip-flops to the ground and jiggles into them. Then she resumes running but she doesn't have to go much farther, just across to the porte-cochère, straight and true as an arrow shot from a bow, into Travis's waiting arms.

Chapter Twelve

Travis catches her in his embrace, and my mind races with panic. What the hell is this kid doing, stalking her across the country?

With an effort of will, I restrain myself. For now. He's come all this way. The least I can do is give them a little privacy.

I offer Travis a greeting that is brief but not unkind. "I'm going for a swim," I tell Molly. "I'll see you in a little bit."

Yes, a swim in the pool. I need to cool off, calm down, clear my head. I don't want to go off halfcocked, say things in haste, jump to conclusions.

When it comes to pools, I'm usually a toe-dipper, getting wet gradually, inch by careful inch. Today I peel off my cover-up and dive off the edge in one swift motion, surrounding myself with a storm of bubbles, hands brushing the gunite bottom. The water is cold but I'm glad for that.

Every nerve ending is wide awake, as I imagine a soldier's would be on the eve of battle.

For me, this is a nightmare—to bring my daughter to the brink of a brand-new, exciting future, only to have the past reach out and pull her back.

Yet for Molly, it's a dream come true. What girl doesn't romanticize about a love so strong, it makes a guy fly across the country just to see her? And in my heart of hearts, I can understand this. We teach our daughters to dream of love. We read them stories of damsels in distress and the knights in shining armor who rescue them, laying happiness at their feet like a carpet of roses.

Of course, in this day and age, we also read about enlightened princesses who do just fine without a man, but those are not the stories that stick with our girls. For some deep-seated, primal reason, the politically correct tales lack appeal. The stories that stay with them always seem to involve a big-shouldered alpha male, sweeping them off their feet.

After a long, vigorous swim, I shower and dress, trying to compose myself. Flying off the handle, yelling, getting mad won't help the situation in the least. I try calling Dan but get voice mail, and hang up without leaving a message. If I try telling his voice mail what's going on I'll use up all our free minutes.

Instead, I head outside to find Molly. She and Travis have been in the shady garden of the motor court, talking and holding each other for a good half hour.

"What's going on?" I ask them. Molly's hair has dried

stiff with chlorine, the curls out of control, her eyes red from crying.

"I had to see Molly," Travis says. His ears are scarlet. I can tell it's hard for him to talk to me.

I struggle to erase all anger and judgment from my stance. "Travis, I understand it was hard to say goodbye. I know you guys miss each other a lot. But it's time—"

"Okay, don't freak out," Molly says. "I have a plan."

To screw up your life. I bite my lip to keep from saying it.

"I'm listening."

"I changed my mind about college," she says, in one short phrase bringing my most negative fantasies out into the open. "I mean, I'll still go. Just not so far away."

"Whoa, hang on. This is a big decision." Brilliant, I tell myself. You're a real rocket scientist.

"It's the right decision." She is instantly defensive. "What I realized this week is that it's too hard, being apart from Travis. I'll be happier at UW."

"Aw, Molly. I know you think that now, but remember, you always wanted—"

"This has never been about what I want," she says, each word slashing like an finely-honed blade. "It's about what you want for me."

"We want the same thing."

"Do we? When was the last time you checked, Mom? This train started out of the station as soon as I got the acceptance letter. It was never, *Do you want this?*"

"I didn't think I had to ask. Forgive me for assuming you wanted to study at one of the best schools in the country and see where it takes you. Forgive me for assuming you worked so hard in high school so you could explore a future beyond the boundaries of a small town."

"I've been thinking about it all week long. We never talked about other options, Mom. We never talked about the fact that one of those options is that I can say, 'Thanks very much, but I have other plans.'"

Travis, never a kid of many words, simply stands there, stalwart and—I can't deny it—impossibly handsome. He shuffles his feet, looks at the message window of his phone as though someone has sent him an answer through the digital ether.

"Tell me about these other plans, Moll. I really want to know."

"The state school makes perfect sense," she insists, her voice as intent and convincing as a trial lawyer's. "It's way cheaper."

"You have a scholarship. One you earned, I might add, all on your own. I didn't make you. This is something you went after because you wanted it."

"And now I want something else." She sends Travis an adoring look, but he's still studying his phone.

The state university is filled with commuter students juggling marriage, motherhood and work in addition to their courseload. No doubt they're gifted, hard-working people who are doing it all, succeeding, living happy and fulfilling lives. Of course the state school is a good option.

Still. It's not the same as the rarefied world of students hand-selected from a pool of the best and brightest, with an endowment big enough to give scholarships to kids like Molly. There will be none of the things we've heard about, no bonfires or late-night study sessions or elaborate pranks, no students from Ghana or visiting lecturers from the UN, no Nobel laureates, no dorm hall dramas or campus productions of the Vagina Monologues, no Parents' Weekend or commencement addresses in Latin.

"I'll get to have what you and I both want," Molly continued. "An education, and Travis."

"There's so much more for you to discover," I tell her, knowing she doesn't believe me.

"Trav and I will discover it together."

I grit my teeth, refusing to let myself explode. "Travis," I say to him, "could Molly and I have a minute?"

"He should stay," she says, clinging to his hand.

"Er, that's okay." He disengages his hand. "Go ahead and talk stuff over with your mom." He steps aside with a conciliatory smile, barely concealing his relief. I almost feel sorry for him, knowing the tension between Molly and me is stretched to its limit, and very palpable. He walks over by the pool and plugs some change into a vending machine.

"Oh, Molly." I pause, trying to find a way to persuade her. "Look how far you've come. Don't give up on something you've been dreaming of for years."

"It's my decision," she says, her eyes welling with tears. "I'm the one who has to go through the next four years. I can either spend them with strangers, struggling to keep up and trying to fit in, thousands of miles from home, or I can be near the people who love me, getting good grades and an education without sacrificing four years of my life."

This sudden streak of practicality is something new. But I can be practical, too. "Most people wouldn't regard a scholarship to a top university as a sacrifice."

"For me it would be. Even this week has been torture," she says. "I *love* him."

Her stark passion gives me pause. What if Travis *is* the one? What if he's the love of her life? It's not as if love comes along every day. Do I have the right to turn her away from him? Suppose she does it my way and tells him goodbye, and something terrible happens? How would I ever forgive myself?

If turning around and going home with Travis is a mistake, it's hers to make, not mine. If it's the right thing to do, then it's only right that she gets to choose.

I can't deny that this unexpected new plan has its appeal. The thought of Molly living in state, coming home with her laundry on weekends, having Sunday dinner with us, draws me in. Yes, I think, yes, that could work, after all.

Still...

Over at the vending machines, Travis has scored a Coke and a bag of Cheetos. He's chatting up the young mom with the two little kids.

Molly sees me rallying a defense. "A college degree...I can get that anytime—anywhere—I want."

"That's what I used to think."

"But Travis. There's only one of him. There are a lot of ways to get a college degree but there's only one Travis."

"And if he loves you, he'll love the dream you're going after."

"If he loves me, he can't stand to be without me. He spent a whole week's pay to fly out here, even."

I bite my tongue to keep from expressing my opinion of *that*. Long ago, I had rationalizations of my own that sounded eerily similar to Molly's. What if she makes the

choice I made? "Sweetie, you're so young. Let yourself *be*
young instead of closing all those doors."

"I can be young with Travis." As though reading my
mind, she adds, "It's exactly what you did, Mom. You went
for love and look how your life turned out. It's wonderful. You and Dad are wonderful. You focused on what's
important."

This is what I've taught her. I've modeled it for her. Go
for the love, every time. It's surprising—and admittedly
gratifying—that she looks at Dan and me and thinks we're
wonderful together. I hope like hell we are.

Yet her insistence on choosing this path still sits poorly
with me. Travis is...just so damn young. He's a good
enough kid, from a nice enough family, but he can be
careless with Molly's feelings, though I've never pointed
that out for fear of starting an argument.

Maybe Dan was that way, too, and I never noticed because I was crazy about him. Now, years later, I sometimes
catch myself wondering, what could I have done, who could
I have been, if I'd gone for the big life instead of the big
love?

Am I making Molly live the life I missed out on? Is that
fair to her?

I gather in a deep breath of courage. "I don't want to
force you into a decision. If you stick to the original plan
and it turns out badly, you'll never forgive me. I'll never
forgive myself. You call the shots, Moll. I'll support you,
no matter what."

"Really? You're not just saying that?"

Maybe. No, I mean it. Molly's life is her own now.

"I mean it."

I feel her strength and determination. She goes to find Travis.

And just like that, that world shifts. The dream changes. Love has transformed her life. Love has a way of doing that.

I call Dan and give him the news. Travis has come for her. He has convinced her to change her mind about going to college so far away. The rundown of Molly's rationalizations spills from me—she claims she can still enroll in the honors program at UW. We won't really forfeit all that much, just this past roller coaster of a week and a percentage of the first tuition payment.

"Says something for the kid, traveling all that way to make his case," Dan tells me.

"What?" I ask, exasperated. "What does it say, Dan? That he's got nothing better to do? That he's ready to take responsibility for her, to hold her heart and her dreams and keep them safe? Or that the plant had a temporary layoff and he got bored hanging out with his friends?"

"Maybe he'll surprise you."

"This is not helping. We need to be on the same page."

"No, we don't. We're two completely different people, and Molly's her own person, too. She's old enough to understand we can have differing points of view."

As we talk, I move around the room, needing an outlet for my agitation. I seize on the bag of quilting supplies. There's a piece made from a pocket with a little embroidered dog on it. This was from the pedal-pushers Molly had worn the day she learned to ride a two-wheeler.

By five years of age, she had worn her training wheels

down to the rims and I insisted it was time to take them off. She had balked, arguing to the point of tears.

She agreed only when Dan promised he would run alongside her, holding her up.

"I won't let go until you say," he vowed.

I was certain she'd never get to the letting-go phase, so I went about my business. I was in the kitchen, trying a new recipe, when I heard shouting and the faint *brrring brrring* of the bell on Molly's bike. I went out to see her cruising on two wheels, Dan standing in the middle of the street and grinning from ear to ear.

"They're young," Dan is saying, "but they're still adults."

"If he was thinking of Molly, then he wouldn't take this opportunity away from her."

"The thing is, it's not up to us—not anymore. Back off, honey. Let Molly work on this herself."

Back off. I can hear Molly's voice—*Oh, like* that's *going to happen.*

I hang up the phone. Something has happened to me over the days of our journey, a subtle shift in the way I see my daughter. She is smart, genuine and more mature than I've given her credit for. Trying to bend her to my will won't work on her any more than it would have worked on me when I was her age. Dan tells me to back off. He has no idea how hard that is. With a heavy sigh, I pick up the quilt where I left off. My needle easily pierces through the layers of cloth and batting, soft beneath the pads of my thumbs. I work in a phrase my mother loved to quote: *To thine own self be true.*

There's a dot of blood on the white underside of the quilt. I didn't notice I'd pricked my finger. I grab an ice cube from the bucket I'd filled earlier and try to get the stain out. It dissolves to a faint rusty shadow but doesn't disappear completely. A bloodstain never does.

After blotting the stain, I set the quilt aside. I don't feel like quilting. I don't feel like anything.

I lie on the bed, staring up at the pockmarked tiles on the ceiling. It's getting late, but I'm not sleepy in the least. Is it my job as a mother to convince her to stay on track for college? No. It's not. It's my job to raise a daughter with an open heart and a good head on her shoulders.

It's a balancing act. Love and dreams and duty. I pick up the quilt again, filled with the softness of memories. All the wisdom in the world is in this quilt.

I stare at it for a long time, wondering if there's anything in it for me.

I wake up in the morning to discover a warm lump of girl curled up against me, under the quilt. She stirs and snuggles closer.

Other memories—all the mornings I awakened her, doing my best to soften the ordeal of getting up for school. I'd lie down next to her on the bed and rub her back until she surrendered to the day. Then I think about all the late nights lying awake, listening for the reassuring rumble of her car engine. We used to have long, whispered conversations when she came in moments after curfew, sitting on the side of the bed to tell me about her date.

Now I marvel at how tender I still feel toward this fully grown creature.

Oh, baby. I used to be responsible for drawing the boundaries around your world. Now you're on a path that leads you over the boundaries and away from me. I'll always cherish our time together. Always. But you'll never be my baby again.

She curls closer, a subtle natural movement, a drawing in. I tuck my arm around her. After a while, she pulls away as though preparing herself for her departure.

"Moll?"

She sighs herself awake. "Yes," she whispers, turning away from me. "This means what you think it means."

"Where's Travis?"

"Where do you think? He went standby on the next flight home."

I exhale a cautious breath of relief. It doesn't last long. Molly comes fully awake, crying with the kind of sobs that shake the whole bed. She's crying too hard to speak, so I just wrap myself around her and hold on for a while, silently willing her to stop. As an infant, she'd been fretful, and I spent many midnight hours walking the floor with her, making mindless shushing sounds, just as I do now.

Eventually, the storm subsides. She is still tearful, her voice shaky. "He was so mad at me, Mom. He was so mad. He might never speak to me again. I hurt him that bad."

"I'm sorry, Moll. I know you can't stand hurting anyone."

"Why couldn't you just let me go home? Why did you have to make a federal case out of it?"

"I left it up to you," I reminded her.

"But it was the *way* you did it. It made me feel like an idiot." Agitated now, she blots her tears with a corner of the quilt and sits up.

"I never meant to do that." But wow, is she right. I want her to have the life I passed up in order to be a wife and mom. She is my road not taken. And it's not fair to put that burden on her. "I'm sorry," I tell her. "If you want to turn around now, we'll do it. No hard feelings, no recriminations."

She's quiet for a long time. "I'd hate myself if I didn't go for this. But I need for you to listen, Mom. This is my choice. I'm not doing it because you never had the chance. I'm doing it because I want the chance for me."

DAY SEVEN

Odometer Reading 123,937

Take your needle, my child,
and work at your pattern;
it will come out a rose by and by.
Life is like that—one stitch at a
time taken patiently and the
pattern will come out all right
like the embroidery.

—Oliver Wendell Holmes

Chapter Thirteen

I hold the map, with the route to the city highlighted. "I think our turn-off is coming up." We pass through suburbs filled with crackerbox houses, small businesses, big-box stores. I notice a fabric shop with a nice window display; maybe I'll stop in on my way back home. There's a charmless strip center with a beauty salon called the Crowning Glory and a charitable organization called New Beginnings, apparently dedicated to providing clothing and supplies for a local women's shelter. There's also a bakery that fills the air with a smell so delicious, it brings tears to my eyes.

We treat ourselves to butterhorns and insulated cups of strong coffee. Molly, always a compulsive reader of free literature, grabs a flyer with a hair salon coupon and a rundown of the women's-shelter services: "Help someone make a New Beginning. Career clothes needed." We try to imagine what it might be like, running for shelter with nothing but the clothes on our backs. It puts our own issues into perspective, for sure, and I keep the flyer, vowing to send a check. We don't linger, though. The destination we've been driving toward for days now lies just a few miles ahead.

We haven't said much about yesterday. Finally, Molly says, "So Travis is home now. He just sent me a text."

I brace myself. She might still want to turn around. "I know you're hurting and I hate that. Everything that happens to you goes straight through my heart."

"Then you know how it feels."

In the beat of hesitation, I hold my breath and wait for her to speak again.

"I have to do this," she says. "I want it, I really do."

"I'm proud of you, Moll. You're going to do great."

We take the interstate to the multilane bridge. Like thick arteries, ramps delve down toward the heart of the city.

An official green-and-white sign marks the city limits. Elevation 40 Feet. Population 101,347.

Molly whips her head toward me. "Which way, left or right?"

"Left."

My thumb traces the route, inching forward as each side street flips past. This place has no grid, just densely aligned roads, some only a block long, others leading nowhere. It's like a web or a net. How will Molly get around in this strange, busy city? How is she going to find her way?

"You have to go left here. Can you make a left from this lane?"

A sense of change takes hold as the city rises around us; I am delivering my only child into uncharted territory. We're here. Our arrival seems abrupt, even though the drive lasted for days. We go from one world to another in a matter of steps. One moment, we're wending our way through a tangle of turnpikes and traffic jams, and the next, we find ourselves in a placid oasis of calm.

The quiet brick street looks like a movie set: trees gracefully shedding the first of their leaves, green rectangular yards crisscrossed by footpaths, colonial-style redbrick buildings with small-paned windows, their frames painted a fresh white. Gaslight fixtures line the sidewalks. The brick walkways bear generations of pockmarks and dents.

We stop and purchase a one-day parking permit. Cars and minivans and SUVs are parked along the curbs on both sides of the roadway. Shiny vehicles disgorge long-legged, laughing girls, slender boys staggering under boxes and cartons, mothers consulting lists, a father or two, standing around talking on cell phones or looking lost.

It's a good thing Dan's not here, after all. He hates feeling like a misfit.

Upperclassmen, facing their orientation groups and talking constantly, are showing the new students around. The tour guides walk backwards with impressive confidence, certain they won't stumble.

Molly maneuvers the rumbling old SUV into the narrow street. It's easily the largest noncommercial vehicle in sight. She pulls into a gap at the curbside, her mouth grim as she tries to align the big truck along the curb. "I won't miss parking this beast," she grumbles.

She switches off the engine. It dies with a shudder. I turn to find her looking at me, and for a moment, the two of us just sit, staring into each other's eyes, not smiling, not talking, just...looking.

It's amazing how much you can see in a face you love, all the layers of years, still visible in the present moment. The infant Molly, her eyes as blue now as they were then, round and open wide, staring upward at me. And my face, eighteen years ago, had filled the baby's whole world.

"Okay," Molly says suddenly, unbuckling her seat belt with a decisive click. "We're here." The car inhales the belt as she jumps out and slams the door.

A black Lexus trolls along the street, headed straight for Molly. *Watch out.* I nearly scream the warning, but the moment passes before I open my mouth. She steps up onto the curb, the car whizzes by and I sit alone in the passenger seat, my heartbeat a stampede of anxiety.

"Okay," I mutter, echoing Molly. "We're here." The breeze carries a subtle chill, a whiff of dry leaves, the tang of autumn. If we were back home, I'd be posting the high school football schedule on the fridge and paging through bulb catalogs.

Molly has the cargo doors open and is staring at the lop-sided stacks and bundles. Uncertainty creases her brow.

I offer a suggestion. "Maybe you'd better—"

"—check in first," Molly finishes for me. "I was *so* going to do that."

"You want me to come in with you?"

"That's okay, Mom. It'll probably only take a few minutes."

"I'll wait out here, then."

The Suburban huddles in a rusty heap, disreputable, inferior compared to the gleaming, late-model cars with plates from Massachusetts, Connecticut, New York, Virginia. In contrast to the forest-green and burgundy imports, the old

Chevy, with its flaking paint job, is as garish and ungainly as a parade float left out in the rain.

The Joads go to college, I'm thinking, certain everyone is staring at me. Glancing in the rearview mirror, I focus on the shopping bag filled with my brand-new, never-worn clothes. I should have worn something special for today, comes the belated thought.

Old worries surface. I still find myself feeling inferior, the misfit, the one who gets picked last. Oh God. Does Molly feel inferior, or did I teach her better? I check her out to see if she's self-conscious about the car. But no. Molly's oblivi-ous as she makes her way inside. She couldn't care less what the car looks like, what state is on the license plate.

I call Dan. I've never been a big fan of mobile phones, but right now, I love my cell phone so much I would marry it. It's proof that someone wants to talk to you. It saves you from having to loiter in a strange place, trying to appear as though you belong.

Molly called him this morning to talk about Travis. He doesn't sound surprised. We backed off and she made her own choice.

"We're here," I tell Dan. "It's amazing."

"How's our girl doing?"

"She didn't have much to say about Travis. We're not talking about it yet. I'm hoping she'll just focus on getting settled here." My gaze skips over the quad, currently an anthill of activity as students move in en masse. "Looks like there's plenty to keep her busy." I take a breath. "Speaking of which, I had a thought."

"Lindy, not another orphan."

"No. Not now, anyway. Saying goodbye to Molly is

making me crazy, I admit it. What I've been thinking about is that I need a new life when I get back."

"Something wrong with your old life?"

"Not at all, but without Molly there, I need a plan. So I thought… Don't freak out."

"I'm listening."

"I'm going to talk to Minerva about the shop."

"What do you mean, talk to her?"

"About taking over the shop. She's retiring, and I thought maybe…I could see if I can qualify for a small-business loan and…" I falter. Spoken aloud, it sounds silly. "Anyway, maybe it's a crazy idea, but I think I can make it work."

Silence.

"Dan?" I wait for him to tell me how foolish I'm being, especially now, with a kid in college.

"You can make anything work, Linda."

It's the last thing I expected to hear from him. "Really?"

"Hell, yeah. Don't sound so surprised."

"But…you never…I never knew you felt that way."

"Sweetheart, I've always felt that way about you. Just because I didn't say it every day doesn't mean the sentiment's not there."

"You were such a skeptic about my last idea—"

"Adopting an orphan? Come on, Linda. This is hardly the same. This is something you want for you, not to fill some void left by Molly."

I shut my eyes, catch my breath. When did I stop knowing this man? I never did; I just let the busy part of life get in the way. *Thank you.*

"I miss you," he says. "I can't wait to see you."

His words ignite a rush of passion in me, an emotion as strong and fresh as the first time I felt it. "Same here," I say, smiling.

Carrying a thick manila envelope, Molly comes out of the dorm, talking to a woman with a clipboard. The woman is about my age, early forties, but she wears her hair in a sleekly careless ponytail and sports an ethnic-print skirt, a trendy blouse and a tooled silver thumbring. Molly looks enchanted with her.

Acutely aware of my lap-creased jeans and the mustard stain on my sweatshirt, I chastise myself again for not wearing a selection from my new clothes. Then I put on my best smile, walk over to the sandstone steps and introduce myself.

"Linda," the woman says, "I'm Ceci Gamble. The residential facilitator." She has a slightly nasal voice and a distinctive, East Coast boarding-school accent.

The theme music of the Wicked Witch of the West buzzes in my head. Who is this exotic new mentor, poised to supplant me? "Nice to meet you. So is Molly all set to move in?"

"Absolutely. Everything's in the information packet. Let me know if you need anything, anything at all."

I smile in gratitude, quashing the sudden resentment, but Ceci Gamble is already turning away, her glossy ponytail flying. She greets another mother who is busy unloading a Mercedes station wagon with a Choate sticker on the back. They crow at each other, embrace, old chums from prep school or the country club. Girls stream past in groups, all talking, the autumn sun strong on their silky, straight hair as they mount the stairs to the freshman dorm.

For a fraction of a second, Molly looks uncertain, her full lower lip soft and vulnerable. She scrunches a hand into her hair. The beautiful corkscrew curls have been the bane of her existence for years, no matter how much her friends claim to covet them. She wishes for straight hair. Prep school hair. East Coast hair.

She's the outsider here, after fitting in so comfortably in high school, playing varsity sports, winning music competitions, laughing on the phone, never at a loss for a friend or a date. She looks lost in the moment now, uncertain. Hesitation is written in her stance, though I'm the only one who can see it. I see the tiny girl afraid to take off her training wheels, jump into a pool, recite a poem for the class, endure her first piano recital, taste an oyster for the first time.

I was always the one pushing her to get past the fear and do it anyway. Dan tended to want to whisk her away from it all. Now I wonder if she felt the constant push-pull of our warring need to protect and promote. Then I remember her confidence in sports, in music, in academics. The gift of her hard work is that self-confidence. She's going to be fine.

I can see her rally in the determined set of her chin. We head inside, to a building that once housed future scientists, jurists, artists and world leaders. Following the directions in the packet, we find a bare room, hung with the smell of Pine-Sol and airless summerlong neglect. Molly heads straight for the window and opens it wide.

The roommate hasn't arrived. Kayla from Philadelphia is nowhere in sight. The barren room contains two phone jacks and wireless modem setups, two desks, twin consoles of drawers and shelves and the requisite two beds. We climb up and down the worn concrete stairs, bringing stuff from the truck to the room. "Want some help unpacking?" I ask.

"That's all right. I'll do it myself. That way, I'll know where everything is." She is clear on not wanting me to linger, to tuck shirts away in drawers, stack office supplies, stand in registration lines with her.

She tackles the first box—towels and toiletries. Then she opens another. Her face looks tense.

"Did you remember your alarm clock?" I ask a mundane question to distract her, but it doesn't work. "Moll?" I ask, tentative, not pushing at all now. "What's up?"

She pulls out the green-shaded desk lamp. "It's broken. I wonder when it broke. Maybe when I slammed on the brakes to miss that deer."

"It can be fixed. We could find a store, look for a replacement for the shade."

"I don't need it."

"You're the one who insisted on bringing it."

"And I was wrong. So sue me. Geez, I can't believe you're still doing this," she snaps.

"Doing what?"

"This... I don't even know what to call it. You want me to be here, to have the whole college experience, but at the same time, you keep acting like I'll fall apart any second. You don't need to fix everything. You don't need to be my human shield anymore. I'm not that fragile. I won't break, I swear. Don't feel like you have to protect me."

"It's my job to protect you."

"Well, congrats. You're finished. Now you can do something else."

The breeze through the open window is reviving her curls.

"Why are you acting so annoyed?" I ask her. I'm getting annoyed, too.

"You always try to make everything easier for me. It's like I live inside this artificial bubble you created. That's what's annoying. It's my time. My life. My turn to screw up and suffer the consequences."

"Your turn to succeed and be amazing."

"Whatever. The point is, it's my turn, Mom. What happened with Travis—just to remind you again, it was my decision. Not yours or Dad's or even Travis's. Mine, a hundred percent. Right or wrong, I own it, okay?"

"Of course."

"So quit worrying." She's close to tears, her expression taut with suppressed panic.

My Molly is terrified. She's afraid she'll be lonely. Afraid she'll fail. Afraid she won't measure up.

"Aw, Moll."

Her shoulders hunch. "What if I blow it? What if I disappoint you?"

Finally, I know what she needs. Maybe this is the whole point of the past week. She needs to be free of the weight of her parents' expectations. "That will never happen."

With a decisive air, she shoves the lamp into a trash can. She looks at me for a long time, her stare penetrating. I try to offer a reassuring smile. She doesn't smile back. Instead, she says, "I'm worried about you, Mom."

It's the last thing I expected to hear. "Worrying is my job."

"No, I mean it. We've had our moments, but you know I think you're great. The thing that worries me is what you're going to do now that I'm gone."

"Don't be silly. I'll do what I've always done."

"What you've always done is be my mom. You need to figure out something else now."

"There's nothing to figure," I say reassuringly. "I have a fulfilling life, great friends, a loving husband. I never defined myself as a mother and nothing else. I have other roles to play."

"Really? Like what?"

"Lots of things. I just have to figure out which roles to pursue. I've been thinking of doing more volunteer work."

Molly clearly notices my lack of enthusiasm. "You should do something you love."

What I love is being your mom. I bite my tongue. I will not lay that on her. Setting my jaw until my back teeth ache, I take out her alarm clock and set it to local time.

Soon we'll be living in different time zones.

"Mom, didn't you used to say you wanted to finish your degree?"

"Yes, but I put it off when I—"

"You put it off," Molly prods.

"I was so busy with everything else, it just wasn't practical. Now it's not important."

"Are you sure? When was the last time you thought about it?"

"Say, I've got an idea—I could get my degree here, while you're here. We could even get an apart—"

"Very funny." Molly's face flashes panic—no doubt she senses I'm only half joking. "Anyway, what's stopping you now?"

"I'm not sure. Lack of ambition, maybe." But there is something I do want, something I have only begun to believe in. "Your dad liked the idea of me taking over Pins & Needles."

"Of course he liked it. It's a perfect idea, are you kidding? You can do anything, Mom. I love the thought of you running the fabric store. I totally love it. I hope you go for it."

Fear and uncertainty turn to something else—Hope. Excitement.

She takes out a small stack of framed pictures, gazes at a shot of her dad with Hoover.

"I know he wishes he could be here," I tell her.

"No, he doesn't. You think I don't know why Dad didn't come?" Molly is incredulous. "You think he stayed home because he doesn't care? He's my father. He didn't come for the same reason he didn't go to the vet with you last spring when Hoover was so sick. It's not weakness or that he doesn't care. It's that he cares too much."

"You know your father well."

"You don't need a college degree to figure Dad out." She sets the photograph on a shelf in her dorm room and her gaze lingers on it. "Look what you're going back to, Mom. How can you not be happy?"

The tension in my chest unfurls on a wave of lightness. I am married to a man with a great heart. My daughter and I both know it.

"Where are you going to eat tonight?" I page through the orientation booklet. "The freshman dining room's in Memorial Hall—"

"Don't worry, Mom. I won't starve. I'm still full from lunch. I might just settle for granola bars and juice."

"You should go to the dining hall, even if you're not hungry." I bite my tongue. I have to stop with the you-shoulds.

I take out the quilt, which I've carefully folded and tied with a ribbon in her high school's colors. "I want you to have this, a reminder of home. It's not really finished, though," I point out. "There's a lot more I wanted to do to it."

"It's great." She unties the ribbon and wafts the quilt over the bed. Sunlight falls across the crazy patchwork, the loopy quilting with its hidden messages.

"It's not finished," I say again, feeling a thrum of panic all out of proportion with the situation. "I thought I would finish it during the trip, and we're here and it's still not done."

"It's beautiful, Mom. I love it."

"I still have to—"

"No, you don't."

"Maybe you could bring it home at Christmas break and I'll work on it some more then."

"Mom, would you stop?" Her sharp tone brings me up short. Out in the hallway of the dorm, we hear a clatter. Then someone shouts, "We need a cleanup on aisle one! I just dropped a blue raspberry slushie." More noise and laughter ensue.

Very slowly and carefully, her hands brushing over the fabric, Molly folds the quilt in half, and half again. And again, revealing the soft, faded underside. She makes a perfect bow with the colored ribbon. "Listen, Mom, don't freak out, okay? But this doesn't belong here, in a dorm room."

"What?"

"I mean, I appreciate it and all, but this is a dorm room. And the quilt is a wonderful, one-of-a-kind work of art. I don't want it to get damaged. I don't want it being used to mop up spilled beer or whatever, not that I would do that but who knows about other kids?"

"You should have it, Moll. See, all the fabric comes from things that are familiar to you, stuff I've saved over the years. It's a keepsake. A picture of your life so far."

"I know, Mom. Believe me, I know. And I love it for that reason," she says. "I love you for making it. That quilt is incredible." She takes a breath, regards me with a wisdom I never knew she possessed. "But it's not my story, Mom. It's yours."

The clarity and wisdom of her words fills me up completely. She's looked at the big picture and seen what I never could. I was so focused on each tiny stitch and detail that I didn't realize what I was creating. What a nutty idea, thinking I could stitch together some kind of patchwork picture of Molly's life so far. It's arrogant, too, to presume to tell her story. Because like she says—it's not a picture of her life. It's a picture of mine. The best part of mine.

"What do you want me to do with it?" I ask her.

"Just don't leave it here where it could get ruined or lost. Keep it for you and Dad…I don't know. Mom, it's so beautiful. It doesn't belong here. Seriously, you know I'm right." She holds the folded quilt out to me, handling it with reverence and respect. "You decide."

I hesitate, then take the quilt from her, holding it against me, knowing my heart is stitched into every square inch of the piece. Each bit of fabric comes from a vanished but

fondly remembered moment in time. All along, I thought it
was about Molly, but ultimately, it is about me—the mother
I was, the moments I remember, the hopes and dreams in
my heart.

But bring it home? What will I do with it then? It'll just
end up in the old cedar chest, stale and forgotten. For me,
the joy of the quilt was in its creation, not in *having* it. But
that doesn't mean Molly's obligated to drag it around.

The last thing she needs is the smothering burden of this
blanket I've patched together, covered with messages from
the past. She wants to create her own story, in her own way,
on her own blank canvas.

That's the daughter I raised.

Chapter Fourteen

"Then…" I shove my hands into the back pockets of my jeans. "I guess I'd better hit the road."

Alarm flashes in Molly's eyes. It's finally real to her. I'm leaving, and she'll soon be all by herself. But she visibly conquers her fear, squelching panic with steely resolve, evident in her posture and the set of her jaw. "Okay," she says. "I'll walk you downstairs."

I turn to conduct one last survey of the place that will be her home for the next year. The room isn't ready. The furniture arrangement isn't ideal. The bookcase is too close to the radiator, and there aren't enough outlets. With every fiber of my being, I want to stay here and fix things, make adjustments, improvements. I force myself to turn away.

The hallway smells of bleach and fresh paint. Someone is mopping up a spill on the floor. Other parents and kids are moving in, some in weighty silence, others with caffeinated chattiness, a few engaged in low-voiced arguments.

"You're not going to lose it, are you, Mom?" Molly asks.

"Yes," I say. "I might."

Molly looks startled. She's used to being protected, shielded, having troubles glossed over and smoothed out so they don't snag on her. But as she pointed out to me earlier, she is a young adult now, old enough to know her mother is not infallible. She swore she didn't need me running interference for her at every turn.

"Check it out," she says, bracing her hands on the windowsill. A cluster of students has gathered in the old yard below. "I think that's the meeting point for the orientation groups. It's geeky, but I kind of want to go."

We step out into the sunny afternoon. I feel a piercing sweetness deep in my heart. A barely dammed river of tears pushes against my chest.

"If you cry," Molly warns, "I'll cry, too."

"Then we'll both cry." And we do, but somehow we manage to stop, regaining control by focusing on the long line of departing cars.

"I've got that orientation meeting," she says, pressing her sleeve across her eyes.

"And I need to get going, too. Maybe miss the traffic heading out of the city."

"That information packet lists some local places to stay," Molly points out. "I mean, if you don't feel like a big drive today…"

"I'm kind of eager to head back to your dad and Hoover," I tell her. What I don't tell her is that I can't face a night at the Colonial Inn with its stupid plaster lamplighters in three-corner hats, knowing Molly is only a short walk away. The temptation to go check on her would be too great and prolong the pain of separation. I plan to drive a couple hundred miles, take a long soak in the hotel hot tub, then phone Molly from a safe distance.

The breeze that sweeps through the quadrangle smells of autumn. A few yellow leaves flutter down with lazy grace. Students and statues populate the ancient, broad lawns laid out centuries before by idealists who embraced order and harmony.

The grassy yard is crisscrossed by walkways littered with new-fallen leaves. Long-bodied boys lie with their heads cushioned on overstuffed backpacks, their noses poked into dog-eared novels. Girls with sweaters draped over their shoulders sit cross-legged in small groups, engaged in earnest debate.

All up and down the street, there is the sound of car doors slamming shut, farewells being called out.

Molly and I walk to the SUV, which is now as empty as an abandoned campsite. My lone suitcase lies in the back alongside the parcel filled with my new clothes. I place the quilt back in its bag and set it down next to the glossy sack from the department store. The thing is coming home with me after all, it seems. Maybe I'll finish it this fall.

"So, okay," Molly says uncertainly. Her eyes dart here and there; she does not look at me. "Thanks for driving with me, Mom. Thanks for everything."

"Sure, honey. Promise you'll call if you need anything, anything at all. I'll have my cell phone on, 24/7." I touch her arm, feeling its shape beneath my fingers. Then I give up pretending to be casual. No point trying to minimize the moment. "Oh, baby. I'm going to miss you so much."

"Me, too, Mom."

Everything I need to say crowds into my throat—eighteen years of advice, guidance, warning, teaching. And it overwhelms me. It is too much…and not enough. Have I forgotten something important? Have I taught her to do laundry and balance her checkbook? To write thank-you notes by hand? Turn off the coffeemaker when it's done? To fend off a horny guy and to contest an unfair grade? To look in the mirror and like what she sees?

There is so much to say. And so I say nothing. There was a time when eighteen years felt like forever, or at least more than enough time to cover every possible topic, but I was wrong about that. I can only hope Dan and I equipped her to make the right choices.

I am amazed to feel something new. I don't want to spout out any more advice or commentary. I want life to happen for Molly in all its pain and joy and richness, revealing itself moment by moment, unfiltered by a mother's intervention. An unexpected, settled feeling creeps in. There are things she knows that will hold and keep her, whether or not I am there. Finally, I'm starting to trust that.

I want her to be on her own. This is what she is supposed to do. It's the natural progression of things. Dan and I have given her everything we have. Now it is time for her to fly, seek new mentors, find her place in the world. I think about all the things that will happen to Molly. Things that will bring her joy and break her heart, make her laugh, cry, rage, exult. I wish I could protect her from the rough parts, but I know I can't. And really, I shouldn't.

The essence of life is the journey, unblunted by an overprotective parent. There is a richness Molly will find even in the deepest sadness. She has a beautiful future ahead of her. Sticking around, interfering and shielding her will rob her of something she needs to figure out on her own. I don't want to stand in the way. Life as it unfolds is just too incredible.

She knows we will always be here for her. Our lives are forever entwined. And yes, she's going to suffer a broken heart and face disappointment and make bad decisions and do all those other things we humans do, but she'll survive them. She's smart and big-hearted and deeply resourceful, probably more than I know, though on this trip I've seen glimpses.

"You're going to be incredible," I finally say. "I'm so happy for you." I am, but I had no idea happiness could hurt so much.

This is it. This is really it. This is goodbye. Suddenly I don't care that there are people all over the place, people who are going to be Molly's friends and neighbors for the next four years. I take my daughter's face between my hands and stare into the eyes I know so well, into a soul that is as bright and clear as the September sky.

She's going to soar, I'm certain of it. Higher than she or I can ever imagine. "Goodbye, Molly," I say. "Goodbye, my precious girl."

Smiling mouth. Trembling chin. "'Bye, Mom."

I kiss her soft cheek, and we embrace, a long strong hug, filled with the wistful scent of autumn and of herbal shampoo. "You are golden," I whisper to my daughter, quoting one of our favorite songs. "You are sunshine." We pull back, smiling, eyes shining.

"I'll call you tonight, okay?" I tell her.

"That'd be great, Mom."

One more kiss. A squeeze of the hands. With slow deliberation, I climb into the truck, roll down the window. We hold hands again while I start the engine. Then I put the car in Drive and let go. Our fingers cling for a heartbeat, then slide apart.

In the rearview mirror I can see Molly standing on the sidewalk, as slender and graceful as the turning trees of the old college yard. Golden leaves fly upward on a gust of wind, swirling around her lone form. My daughter stands very still, and just as the truck turns the corner onto the busy avenue, she raises one hand, waving goodbye.

Tapping the horn to acknowledge the wave, I let out a breath I didn't realize I was holding.

I set the iPod to a mix of quiet songs. The first one is a classic, from my dating days with Dan. As the music plays, I head for the interstate, tears still escaping to soak into the neckline of my sweatshirt. I flex my hands on the steering wheel, set my jaw. So what if I'm crying. I'm the mother. I get to cry if I want to.

The traffic flows like a viscous liquid, undemanding, carrying me swiftly away from the city, the car a fallen leaf in a rushing stream.

As the city fades away behind me, I picture Molly in her freshly painted dorm room, unpacking her belongings, putting her new sheets on the narrow iron-frame bed, propping up snapshots of her friends and family, her dog and Travis, shelving books and supplies, plugging in the computer, organizing her things. Eventually she will come across the covered plastic box I filled with her favorite snacks— microwave popcorn, granola bars, Life-savers, pecan sandies, canned juices, cinnamon-flavored gum. Inside she will find a familiar note scribbled on a paper napkin: a little smiling cartoon mommy, with squiggles to represent the hair, and a message that will remind her of all the homemade lunches of her childhood: "I ♥ U. Love, Mommy."

I think about giving Dan a call and I will, but not just yet. This moment is too raw, but it's mine to feel—the bittersweet triumph, the sadness, the hope. On this leg of the journey, there will be no detour or scenic route as I make my way home.

Home, to Dan, who said he can't wait to see me. Home, to a life that is open like the pages of an unread book. *Yes*.

I'm ready to live my life. Okay, maybe I'm a little scared, but in a good way. I want to discover who I am on my own, what I love beyond the obvious, and what I really want for the rest of my life.

At the west end of the city, I pass a suburban strip mall I remember from the day before, with the Crowning Glory Salon, the delicious-smelling Sweet Dreams bakery and the charity called New Beginnings. The charity is closed for the day but there's a big metal donation box in the front. Under the Web address for the charity is its slogan: "Comforting women and children in need."

On impulse, I turn into the parking lot, go around to the back of the Suburban and open the gate. Molly's observation drifts back to me: This is about *your* life, Mom.

I stand there for a minute, thinking about the woman I've been for the past eighteen years and wondering who I'll be for the next eighteen. It's a bit scary to contemplate, but exciting, too.

When I grab the parcel, my resolve wavers. Then I think, go for it. The true meaning of charity is to give freely, no strings attached. I have to let go, only trusting that my gift will be out there in the world somewhere, doing whatever it's bound to do.

And then I push the bag into the drop box, having to shove its soft bulk inch by inch through the narrow slot. At first I worry that it won't go down the chute, and I have to push hard. Then the last bit slips through easily and disappears.

Stenciled under the chute are the words, "Thank you for your donation."

I return to the still-running car. Something stirs inside me, a sensation as empty and light as the curling, cup-shaped leaves lifted by the autumn wind.

Stopping at the last red light before the on-ramp to the interstate, I catch the blinding beam of the late afternoon sun in my eye. The days of summer have grown shorter. The year is getting old already.

I flip down the sun visor, and a stray slip of paper drifts into my lap. Picking it up, I unfold it and see a little smiling cartoon face, corkscrew squiggles for hair, and a note that says, "I ♥ U. Love, Molly."

Epilogue

The shop called Pins & Needles looks the way it always has, since its founding decades ago. Its brick and concrete façade glows in the evening light, the windows framed with swaths of fabric. The holidays are past and winter has settled in. The air is sweet and dry with the peculiar clarity that the winter cold brings. The shop is open late tonight, but there is no business to be done.

In the window is a hand-lettered sign: "Retirement Party. Come celebrate with us."

Standing behind the counter, I feel as if I'm glowing, too, with a sense of happiness and fulfillment. All around me are my customers, the women who frequent the shop, talking together and sharing all the events of their lives. They've brought platters of cookies and a crystal bowl filled with punch. Minerva, now in a wheelchair, beams at me. "It's a good time to move on, eh?"

"I can't believe it's been twenty-five years," says my best

friend, Erin, as she gives me a hug. "Happy retirement, Linda."

I can't believe it either, sometimes. All those years ago, when I struggled with myself after taking Molly to college, the answer was staring me in the face. I didn't need a bag full of gorgeous new clothes to find my new life. They did more good giving someone else a fresh start; donating the brand-new things to the women's shelter was the right thing to do. Dan loves me as I am. The women at Pins & Needles do, too. I just needed to be the person I've always been—a wife, a friend and neighbor, a needleworker, a dabbler.

The proof is here before me now, a warmhearted shop filled with women I've come to know like sisters through the years. Minerva, who celebrated her ninetieth last year, has been my mentor. As the festivities go on, Molly and her husband arrive, their three kids in tow, and suddenly my arms are filled with grandchildren. The sweetness of this moment makes my heart expand with joy. Dan comes over, laughing about being outnumbered by females. He's as strong and handsome as the day I met him nearly fifty years ago, wearing his age like a fine patina. He raises a cup of punch to me. "I knew you could do it, but now I can't wait to have you all to myself." Still a man of few words, he retreats with our son-in-law to forage for snacks and to escape the chattering women.

After Molly left for college, I missed her terribly, but my life took a new turn and opened up in new ways. I found a dream of my own and went for it. Running the quilt shop didn't make me a rich woman, not in the financial sense. But it enriched my life beyond measure, and I can see that so clearly now, looking around at the faces of my family and friends, customers and well-wishers. The big changes can't be seen, only felt.

Molly gives me a hug and steps back, her eyes shining. "Happy retirement, Mom. I'm really proud of you."

Her words light me up like sunshine, as they always have. We turn together to the display wall behind the counter, regarding the quilt, the one I was making for Molly so long ago. She had it right all along—it *was* my story, and it wasn't finished.

Family. History. Love and loss. I've touched every inch of this fabric. It's absorbed my scent and the invisible oils of my skin, the smell of our household, the occasional drop of blood, and sometimes my tears. I've added to the piece through the years; it's an ever-expanding record of our days as a family. There's a swatch from Molly's graduation gown, and a ribbon from the table decorations on her wedding day. There's a piece from her husband's desert fatigues, and little precious bits from my grandchildren. A tiny silver bell marks our twenty-fifth wedding anniversary. I'm already wondering what little symbol will commemorate our golden anniversary. I try not to plan ahead. Why rob life of its surprises?

I plan to take the quilt home with me tonight, and no doubt more keepsakes will make their way into the design. Life has taught me not to be afraid of starting something new.

How do you say goodbye to a piece of your heart? You don't ever have to. There's always a way to keep the things we hold most dear.

* * * * *

ACKNOWLEDGMENTS

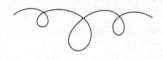

I'm very fortunate to have a publisher that allows me to put my heart on paper. Many thanks to my editor and great friend, Margaret O'Neill Marbury, and to everyone at MIRA Books. As always, I'm indebted to Meg Ruley, Annelise Robey and their associates at the Jane Rotrosen Agency—your wisdom, patience and friendship mean the world to me.

To my fellow writers—Anjali Banerjee, Kate Breslin, Carol Cassella, Sheila Roberts and Suzanne Selfors—thank you so much for reading multiple drafts and helping me pull this patchwork of emotion together.

I'm grateful to master quilter Marybeth O'Halloran for the insights and expertise into her colorful world—any liberties and errors in the text are my own. A very special thank-you to my dear friend, Joan Vassiliadis, for creating the original Goodbye Quilt and for sharing her talent in the pages of this book.

The Goodbye Quilt Pattern

by Joan Vassiliadis

www.joanofcards.blogspot.com

Finished size is approximately 45" x 56"
Instructions based on 42" wide fabric
All seams are ¼"

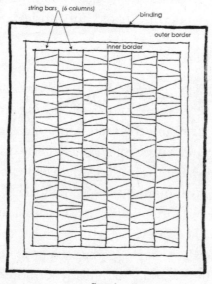

Figure 1

Fabric Requirements

Collect 100% cotton fabric scraps that have special meaning to you. Don't be afraid to cut into old things. You will be able to enjoy them much more in a quilt that will be seen and touched every day. Make sure your scraps are at least 7" wide and total approximately 2 ½ yards. Inner border: ½ yard solid color to frame the string bars. Outer border: 5/8 yard. Backing: 3 ¼ yards. Binding: ½ yard.

Cutting Instructions

Cut approximately 220 strings all 7" in length—cut uneven widths ranging between 1" and 3". Inner solid border: cut 4 strips crosswise (from selvage to selvage) 2 ½" wide. Outer border: Cut 4 strips crosswise 4" wide. Binding: Cut 2 ½" strips to total the perimeter of your finished quilt.

Sewing Instructions

Play music while you work, sing along and remember why each piece of fabric is special to you. Begin constructing the bars first into pairs and then into fours and so on. Put dark colors next to light if possible, but don't worry too much about it if you have more darks than lights or vice versa. Do be careful to pin and press. Whenever possible, press towards the dark fabric. Construct six bars at least 44" long. Your edges will be uneven so trim each bar to 6" wide (see Figure 2). Sew all six bars together and press. Trim the ends so they are all even and you're ready for borders.

For the inner border, measure your quilt lengthwise first, and construct two strips 2 ½" wide to this length. Sew to the sides of the quilt and press. Next, measure the width of your quilt. Construct two strips 2 ½" wide to this measurement. Sew to the top and bottom of the quilt and press.

Now for the outer border: Measure the sides of your quilt and construct two strips 4" wide to this length. Next,

measure the width of your quilt. Construct two strips 4"
wide to this measurement. Sew to the top and bottom of
the quilt and press. Your top is now complete! Think about
all of the memories sewn into this quilt...remember the
sweetest moments of life.

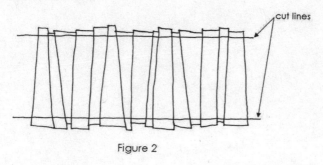

Figure 2

Finishing the Quilt

Linda finished her quilt on the drive with Molly. You can
finish yours in the car, in a comfy chair, with your quilting
friends at the dining-room table...any way and anywhere
you please! If tying your quilt you can embellish with more
memories: buttons, ribbons, badges. Do think about how
often your quilt will be washed and how your embellishments will endure. If you make your quilt an art piece,
then you can incorporate almost anything. After quilting,
measure the perimeter and sew binding strips together to
total this measurement. Attach binding.

You're invited…
To celebrate love, happiness and new beginnings.
Read the exclusive excerpt from
HOW I PLANNED YOUR WEDDING
by Susan Wiggs and Elizabeth Wiggs Maas.
Susan Wiggs and her daughter pull back the veil on how a
mother and daughter really plan a wedding together…

ONCE UPON A TIME... THE JOURNEY BEGINS

ELIZABETH

I was born to be a bride. There are family photographs of me in a bridal gown dating all the way back to age two. Even in my imagination, every detail was precisely arranged—the flowers, the veil, the tiara, the sparkly shoes, the smear of lipstick across my mouth. But in those little-girl fantasies, there was one small missing detail: the groom.

Then, senior year of college, the heavens opened up, angels sang from on high and one tipsy night I found myself alone with Dave. I'd seen him around school before (after all, there were only 1,500 students at our tiny liberal arts college), but something about him was...different. Specifically, he looked like a god. Over the summer, he'd grown his glossy, blond hair past his shoulders and had sprouted an extra six inches in height, taking him to a towering 6-foot-4. Pair that with his gracefully lean cross-country runner's body and I'd bagged myself the offspring of Brad Pitt and a Thomson's gazelle.

During that first fateful night in his dorm room when we had, ahem, chastely chatted from opposite ends of the futon, he asked if I wanted to brush my teeth, to which I replied "Hell, yes" because, you know, stale cheap beer breath isn't the most romantic thing in the world. As soon as our pearly whites were clean and fresh, Dave looked at me and began slowly leaning in, a gentlemanly question in his eyes, waiting for my signal that, yes, he could now storm the citadel on his steed, breaching the gates of my... well, you know. I'm not one for subtlety, so I grabbed him by the ears and yanked him into the make-out session to end all make-out sessions. And that's about all I'm going to say about *that,* Dear Readers. I'm collaborating with my *mother* on this project, after all.

As it turns out, that was the *last* "first" kiss I would ever share with a man, though I didn't know it at the time. I certainly hoped so, because it was *that* magical, the kiss that erased all others. The defining smooch. The zing of chemistry between Dave and me was palpable. After growing up under the wing of a bestselling writer, I finally, *finally* understood what my mom's books were really about—and why they're so addictive to so many readers. Dave and I spent countless hours talking and cracking each other up, falling under that magical spell that has launched a million romance novels.

Exactly three years, seven months and twenty-two days later, I would kiss this same dude in a sunlit, fountain-fed atrium full of our family and friends: our first kiss as husband and wife. But between that first Pabst Blue Ribbon–fueled make-out session and the moment we sealed our marriage with a kiss, we had a mountain to climb. A mountain of friggin' insane wedding planning that would, no matter how we fought it, be heavily supervised and directed by a woman who creates over-the-top, happily-ever-after romance for a living: my mom.

SUSAN

Of all the dreams I ever dreamed for my daughter, the biggest one was the dream in which she finds the one person in the world who will love her for the rest of her life. Because, after all, love in all its forms gives life its meaning. I've always believed that. I'd *better* believe that. I've made a career out of it, after all.

But when it comes to real-world matters, there's a deeper reason for wanting your child to spend the rest of her days with the love of her life. It's the one secret you can't tell her. She has to find out for herself. A lasting love is the deepest of life's joys.

When Elizabeth was very little, and people asked what she wanted to be when she grew up, she didn't say a teacher or a doctor, an artist or a sales clerk or a hot-air balloon pilot.

She would tell them, "A bride."

My friends would offer pitying looks. "I'm so sorry. She'll grow out of it. She'll realize that what she really wants is to be a rocket scientist or a chef or a choreographer..."

I didn't really need their pity, and I wasn't bothered by her oft-stated aspiration. As a romance writer, I never quibbled with her dream. Of course she wanted to be a bride. She wanted to find the man of her dreams and live happily ever after.

Is there any higher calling? Any bigger dream?

And so I let her fantasy grow and develop, unimpeded by other people's expectations or even common sense. The vision was embellished with horse-drawn carriages made of crystal, a banquet consisting of nothing but French toast, Skittles and spun sugar, a ball gown so elaborate it wouldn't even fit through doorways. The bride would be attended by her best and most beautiful friends, including her Airedale terrier.

When it came time to plan her actual wedding, this vision stayed more or less intact. Sure, the horse-drawn carriage morphed into a white stretch limo, complete with glittering disco lights in the ceiling, and the family dog had gone over the rainbow bridge, but overall, her dream came true—the gown, the beautiful friends, the hair, the pearls...

But where does that leave me, the mom?

I'm not quite sure how to say this, so I'll be blunt. Does anybody actually dream about being the *mother* of the bride?

Come on. That's kind of like getting stuck with Midge—the sidekick—while playing Barbies. It's also sure to mess with your denial about exactly how old you are.

Hello? You are now old enough to actually have a daughter who's getting married. A new generation has come along, and here you thought *you* were the young generation. You didn't even notice the runner behind you, reaching forward to pass you the baton.

Deal with it. No, do better than that. Embrace it. And don't forget to savor the process. After all, that's what you've been doing all her life, I suspect.

If you're like me, the mother of an adored and indulged child who has owned your heart for the past twentysomething years, you remember every single minute. You remember what her toddler voice sounded like when she laughed. You remember the little-girl smell of her, and dresses that were too expensive but you bought them anyway because you just had to see her in that adorable smocked pinafore. You remember the feel of her tiny—usually sticky—hand in yours as you took her into unfamiliar situations: A swimming pool. Kindergarten. The IMAX. A petting zoo. Her first piano recital. The dentist. You remember the victory dance she did to celebrate accomplishments from winning a race in a swim meet to learning cursive writing in the third grade. You remember laughing so hard your sides ached, and holding her when she cried, willing to trade your soul to keep her from hurting. You remember how much she loved goodnight kisses, how much she hated black olives, and how very sure she was that you would always be the center of her world.

And then, before you know it, this poised and accomplished young woman appears—seemingly out of nowhere—with a young man at her side. And not just any young man. *The* young man. Prince Charming. The forever guy.

They have Big News. They can't wait to tell you. Turns out Prince Charming has even been conspiring with your husband, arranging the surprise proposal, the whirlwind romantic weekend, the start of plans that are about to consume you for the next sixteen months.

All right, so you're not the center of her world anymore. You're the Mother of the Bride. Even the phrase itself makes you sound old. Dowdy.

But here's a secret: you're in for the time of your life.

THE ONE

Not the man, silly—the dress. Dress shopping and the
hunt for the last frock you'll ever wear as a single gal

ELIZABETH

My quest for the dress began with a mistake. Dark forces
were at work, inexplicably drawing me to the swankiest
bridal salon in Seattle, a place that would eventually prove
to be more toxic than the set of VH1's *Rock of Love*. (For the
uninitiated, that's one of the finest reality shows on televi-
sion, in which a troupe of strippers with balloons for breasts
compete for the lust of aging rock musician Bret Michaels.)

In fiction, such places are guarded by rabid, three-headed
dogs, but at the Swank Salon (names changed to protect the
bitchy), Cerberus had been replaced by a burbling replica
of the Trevi Fountain.

My mom, my future bridesmaid, Molly, and I skipped
happily through the flower- and crystal-encrusted door into
a hippodrome-sized, airy room filled with every beautiful wedding gown I ever imagined. I'd never given much
thought to the infinite possible shades of white, but here I
was, jaw on the floor, confronted by the whole pale spec-
trum gleaming in satin and silk, lace and lamé. The shop
was designed in the round, with layers of dresses lining the
outer walls of the space like a cupcake wrapper, tasteful

doors with hand-painted French signs tucked away behind the racks. Each door was unique, and promised a cozy and beautiful nook for trying on the dress of my dreams.

But the center of the store was what really made me need the crash cart.

There, raised about three feet off the chic navy-blue carpet, was a glowing Lucite runway. Plush ivory chairs sat at either end of the runway, understated yet unspeakably elegant, with crystal champagne glasses on low tables and bottles of Dom Perignon chilling in monogrammed ice buckets. A discreet video camera was set up at the far end and live images of the empty runway appeared on flat-screen televisions throughout the shop. French music from the movie *Amélie* filled the air, just soft enough to add to the ambience without interrupting the rustle of chiffon and tulle.

I felt a string of drool dribble from my lower lip and plop on the old tank top I wore.

"We'll give you a DVD of all the dresses you try on, so you can show anyone in your life who's not here today," cooed voice behind me, dripping with sweetness.

I turned around and stared down at the waif of a salesgirl who had materialized behind me like a silent-but-deadly fart.

"I'm Brigitte," she said.

Her black hair was meticulously teased into an edgy, bouffant-style ponytail. Her eyes were expertly rimmed in kohl black eyeliner, adding drama to her pale, elfin face and petal-pink cheeks. She smiled at me, revealing a row of perfect teeth that were whiter than any of the dresses she peddled. She wore black skinny jeans and a beige cashmere sweater that wrapped luxuriously around her small form as though it had been made for her. When she moved, a collection of chic bangles on her wrists made a soft clanging noise, calling attention to her perfectly manicured, purple-black fingernails. She probably weighed about the same as one of my calves.

In short, she was a bride's worst nightmare. She pretty much looked like a model, except she wasn't tall so I couldn't convince myself that she was one of those girls who's too tall to love (I get judgmental when I'm feeling intimidated). I quickly realized that I would be trying on my dresses in front of her, which didn't bode well for my self-esteem. Standing next to her, I felt like the offspring of a cow and an ogre. The cellulite on the backs of my thighs tingled a warning signal at me, as if to say, "Get out while you still have your dignity!"

But I didn't listen. The siren call of the runway in the center of the enormous shop was too much for me. I sucked in my gut, plastered a confident-ish smile on my face and introduced myself.

She looked me slowly up and down, one delicate hand twirling a silky strand of dark hair. She frowned slightly, her impeccably waxed eyebrows coming together in an expression of thoughtful confusion. I could practically hear what she was thinking: What could possibly disguise those flabby arms without accentuating her pear-shaped hips? (This was before I had gotten in shape for the wedding, after all. But still.)

"What do *you* think would look best on you?" she asked me. The emphasis on *you* made it seem like she very much doubted my fashion sense. I mean, I was wearing old yoga pants and a shirt with a built-in bra, but isn't that what most gals would wear when planning to spend an entire day trying on dresses?

I'm just glad I'd been planning my wedding gown from the moment I popped out of the womb, because I had a firm answer for her: "I want the biggest ball gown you've got. Strapless."

She smiled, her glossy lips turning up even as her eyes lingered on my upper arms as if to remind me that a strapless gown would do nothing to hide the lard-filled wings that flopped from my biceps whenever I moved.

I reminded myself that from her point of view, in which Kate Moss represented the ideal body type, my slightly undefined triceps muscles would appear offensively large. And, yes, I did need to do more dips at the gym. But I was a former college athlete, and I knew how to get myself toned. Sure, I could stand to lose ten pounds or so, but I tried to remember that I wasn't as grossly obese as her expression implied. A strapless gown would look lovely on me. I might just need to live on celery and water for a month before the wedding.

I smiled back. "Yep," I said. "A strapless ball gown."

"Great!" she chirped. "And what budget are we working with?"

As she asked, she began to usher my mom, Molly and me to a corner of the store where I could see deliciously poofy-looking skirts dangling beneath delicate-boned bodices.

"Uh…I was thinking maybe around a thousand bucks? I guess I could go up to fifteen hundred if it was perfect enough. Does that sound about right to you, Mommy?"

I looked at my mom and Molly, hoping that I hadn't just named an offensively outrageous sum of money.

"Or *less*," my mom stated, seemingly unfazed by this evil bird of a woman.

The heroin-chic salesgirl stopped in her tracks. I could practically hear the soles of her patent-leather ballet flats screech on the floor. With a poisonous look in her eyes, she rounded on me.

"I'm not sure if you know how much a *high-fashion dress* costs in an upscale shop like ours, but you *really* need to reconsider how much you're willing to spend on the *most important gown you'll ever wear*." The bangles on her wrists jangled as she stabbed her tiny hands through the air to emphasize her point.

Suddenly, she looked down and stopped midsnarl. I saw her eyes light on my mom's robin's egg blue Christian Louboutin pumps (bought for 90 percent off their usual $900 price tag at Nordstrom Rack). The sight of high-end shoes seemed to calm her.

"I mean," she tittered, taking on the tone of a concerned friend, "you wouldn't want to pass up the gown of your dreams just because you're letting a *silly little thing* like budget get in the way, would you?"

"I…I…" I stammered.

I think I was suffering from temporary insanity due to couture vapors, because if I were treated this way in any other circumstance, I would have flashed her my pleasantly plump middle finger and gone out for a burger. But here, in this tulle-draped shop that looked as though it had been spun from my little-girl wedding dreams, I was speechless.

Brigitte saw my moment of weakness and knew she had

me. All she had to do was get past my last line of wedding defense—my mom.

She looked down at my mom's shoes as if to gather strength from their signature red soles, then tried a new tactic: "Mrs. Wiggs, I can see by your ensemble that you're a woman who knows fashion. You must see how *tragic* it would be for your daughter to wear a less-than-perfect gown on the day of her wedding."

My mom, in an uncharacteristic moment of gullibility, seemed to waver. I'm guessing this resulted from the cloying scent of gardenias wafting through the air from the multitude of floral arrangements adorning the shop.

"Well," she said, "I suppose we could look at a couple of *slightly* more expensive gowns…but nothing over two thousand. I'd be shocked if we can't find something beautiful for such a price."

The words *more expensive* seemed to bring Brigitte back to life. Invoking a salesgirl's selective deafness, she ignored the *slightly* part of my mom's response and promptly took us on a whirlwind tour of tulle-and-satin heaven. She seemed to float around the shop, hoisting piles of gowns that must have weighed more than she did and transporting them to a dressing room that resembled Marie Antoinette's boudoir.

She ordered me to strip down to my grundies (that's grandma-undies, to those of you who are still convinced that G-strings are comfortable). It only took me a minute (and a glass of Dom Perignon) to forget my jiggly abs and flabby butt as dress after beautiful dress slipped over my head, each more stunning than the last. Brigitte's fingers flew, fastening rows of minuscule hook-and-eye button closures with machine-like speed; she was able to fill my mom's and Molly's champagne flutes with little more than a threatening glance. Finally, when I thought I had been through every ball gown the store had to offer, Brigitte opened the door to my dressing room. "I saved the best for last," she breathed, a glint in her eye.

With the wily skill of a crack dealer, she produced a breathtaking whisper of couture for me, reverently placing the cloudlike garment on a gilded hook on the wall. She whisked aside my privacy curtain without so much as a "Hide your eyes" to Molly or my mom. "You'll want to see this one, ladies," she said.

I tried to pull a Venus-on-a-half-shell maneuver with my hair and my hands, hiding my lady bits as much as possible, but my pathetic attempt at modesty was unnecessary as all eyes in the dressing room were on the silk tulle layers of the gown. As it swayed on its hanger, I noticed subtle crystals peeking through the folds in the voluminous skirt. Swoon.

Employing a device that looked like a giant crowbar, Brigitte forced me to pour my pre-wedding-diet hips into the size 0 and had the buttons fastened down my back before my flesh could burst free. I was disconcerted. Vaguely humiliated, even. I felt like a sausage whose casing was too small.

I turned, disappointment on my face, to Molly and my mom. "I look like a joke, don't I?"

Molly's eyes were like saucers. "Oh, Wiggs," she said, her eyes full of emotion.

I knew it. I knew it! Brigitte's hard stares at my winter-soft physique hadn't simply been the result of her lifelong goal to be able to hide behind a toothpick. Sure, she hadn't actually said anything about my body, but I knew what she was thinking, and she was right. Now Molly thought so, too.

I should just get married in a bathrobe. I could never pull off the ball gown I'd been dreaming of since I could say "printheth" in my toddler's lisp.

I glanced at my mom and saw her clutching her heart.

Okay, it wasn't that bad, was it?

Was I really giving my mom heartburn with my over-the-top wedding dress preferences?

I turned slowly to look in the mirror and survey the damage. There, standing before me, was exactly what I'd been fantasizing since I was a little girl.

The dress was...perfect. The skirt drifted to the floor, forming a large bell with a four-foot train that would have made Disney animators jealous. The bodice nipped in at the narrowest part of my waist and suddenly I found myself glad for my curvy hips. The warm ivory color of the delicate tulle set off creamy peach tones in my skin, causing my blue eyes to take on a cerulean hue. My hair, pulled carelessly back and slightly frizzy from the frenzy of dress changes suddenly seemed carefree and romantic. A soft sweetheart neckline, bordered by glinting crystals, gave me nontrashy cleavage (how's that for a miracle?), and huzzah! My arms looked slender.

The skinny bitch got it right. This dress was The One.

I happily skipped about the entire store, jumping up on the runway and flouncing to and fro, checking myself out in the mirrored walls and squealing like a contestant on *The Bachelor.*

I looked Brigitte in her flat eyes and said, "This is it. I'll take it."

In a flash, her face came to life and her expression changed to what can only be described as a barracuda with a plump, juicy goldfish in its sights. "Great," she cackled, steepling her fingers (seriously, she really did steeple her fingers). "This one is $12,000. Plus tailoring, fitting, prewedding storage, dewrinkling, steaming, refitting, day-of fitting, postwedding storage." She might as well have added postdivorce repurposing for good measure.

I'd been waiting for my mom to burst into tears when I found the dress of my dreams. And she did, but I'll never know if it was the sight of her little girl in the bridal gown, or the price tag that broke her down.

My lower lip began to tremble. Twelve *thousand* dollars? But that was almost my entire wedding budget! Wildly, my mind began to race, trying to divine a way for me to afford the gown. *You could have this dress if you fed your guests squirt cheese on Rye Crisps and downgraded the music to a kazoo quartet,* I told myself.

You could offer to moonlight here as a salesgirl and work off some of the cost, I thought. I looked at Brigitte and realized I'd never make it in the underworld.

Then I was hit by a lightning bolt of genius. *Run!* I heard the voice in my head screaming. *Run now! While she's not expecting it!* As my leg muscles tensed, I was already calculating how much jail time I could get for stealing a $12,000 dress. I edged toward the door, trying to recall exactly where I'd parked the getaway car. And then I caught another glimpse of myself in the mirror—this time from across the room, where the fine details on the dress (including the designer's name embroidered into the tag) weren't as apparent.

You know what I looked like?

A bride. A bride in a big, white dress. A young, excited bride who was glowing with happiness over the prospect of decades spent with her soul mate.

The expression on my face—the one I'd been wearing since I met Dave, actually—was the most stunning part of my ensemble, and I knew then that any gown I chose for my wedding day would simply be icing on the cake. But it wasn't the cake. *I* was.

Because, folks, here's the reality: a big white dress is a big white dress. It doesn't matter if it was designed by Coco Chanel or Koko the Ape. Other than the occasional Rachel Zoe addict, no one is going to be able to tell the difference. Cheesy as it sounds, a happy bride's smile will shine more brightly than any Swarovski crystal ever could.

So go ahead and wear your dress (or skirt, or pantsuit, or bikini, or skort or whatever bridal outfit you choose) like it came right off a Parisian runway. The only thing people will remember (if they remember anything besides the color) is how you glowed with joy. And maybe some will remember the cut (including you), so if you want a ball gown, get a blasted ball gown because it's the only chance you'll have to wear one without looking like you're in a costume.

If you find your dream gown and it's in your price range, more power to you. I wasn't so lucky. But that dress set the bar. As I happily flounced out of the snobby store, taking with me any commission Brigitte could have hoped to earn, I had to thank her for one thing: she gave me exactly what I was looking for—a vision quest. I had been within reach of The Dress, and all that remained was for me to find something equally gorgeous with a price tag that wouldn't require me to sell a kidney. From then on, my dress shopping would be efficient and focused. I would only consider ball gowns, and only those under a thousand bucks.

Everything happens for a reason, my mom says. Looking back, I can see now that without the encounter with Brigitte, I never would have ended up at the next shop.

Later that afternoon, my mom, Molly and I went to lunch in the quaint neighborhood of Wallingford in Seattle. Molly spent a good part of the lunch convincing me to eat more than a piece of lettuce, reminding me that I was not actually a candidate for world's largest woman and that I was *definitely* not allowed to let Brigitte and her skeletal aesthetic make me feel bad about myself. My mom simply said in her most matter-of-fact voice, "You can't trust a girl who weighs less than the purse she carries."

As we walked out of the café, I glanced across the street. Nestled along a rosy pink wall, four shop windows displayed mannequins in long, white gowns. Above the door to the small shop, a humble black awning read, I Do Bridal.

I'll be honest with you. I always pictured finding my gown in a place that oozed upscale elegance. My dressing room attendant would serve my mom and bridesmaids teacakes and champagne as I tried on dress after beautiful dress, emerging from behind a billowy silk curtain to stand on a dais in front of the women in my life as they lounged on a pillow-soft couch. Even after my experience with The Harpy Formerly Known as Brigitte, I figured I'd find another store with a similar atmosphere—and more reasonable prices.

I Do Bridal looked a little…homemade, compared to my fantasy.

This is where it came in handy to have an insanely practical mother and a down-to-earth bridesmaid with me.

"Wiggs, why don't we try that shop?" Molly asked. She knew a thing or two about finding wedding dresses in unlikely places. Her own wedding was a mere two months away, and she would be wearing an incredible raw silk A-line gown she'd found in an eastern Washington quinceañera shop that sported a window display of neon-green prom dresses.

My mom piggybacked onto this: "Yeah, it looks like the exact opposite of the last place. It will be a breath of fresh air."

Feeling grumpy and tired, I turned up my nose. "I'm not going to find what I'm looking for in *that* place," I sneered. "'I Do Bridal?' How about 'I Do Saks Fifth Avenue?'" I huffed, thinking myself clever.

But Molly and my mom already had me by the wrists.

They bodily threw me through the door. The first thing I saw was a tattered, industrial-style carpet littered with small threads, sequins and buttons that had fallen off sample dresses. In one corner stood a fake-gilt fainting couch for the moms. The air was musty, and as I looked up, I saw why: on three racks crammed into a space roughly the size of Dave's 1980 two-door Volvo sedan, a mountain of wedding dresses threatened to explode from their tight confines like my back fat from a size 0 bodice.

I stifled a groan and mentally vowed to appease my mother by trying on three token dresses before I made a beeline for the car.

"Hi!" chirped a cheerful voice. Emerging from the nest of dresses like a bridal gnome, a small woman beamed at me. She looked...well, like me, only Asian. Young, with an average build, wearing comfortable jeans and a T-shirt, her glossy black hair pulled back into a low ponytail. She wore no makeup and had a genuine smile, and as she reached out to shake my hand I noticed a small but beautiful solitaire engagement ring on her finger. "I'm Bridget," she said.

I immediately liked her. I looked around to see if someone was playing a joke on me—she really was the non-French version of the snob from the first store. My mom and Molly smiled at each other, knowing how serendipitous this was. It seemed like a sign.

I resolved to keep an open mind—even though the entitled bride-devil on my shoulder kept whispering sweet nothings in my ear about expansive dressing rooms and Oscar de la Renta gowns. I calmed myself down by promising to make an appointment with Saks immediately if the dresses here were lame.

I told Bridget that I wanted the biggest dress she had. She congratulated me on my engagement and asked me a couple of questions about the wedding, my dress budget, my style and, most importantly—what my fiancé wanted me to wear. "Obviously, he doesn't get the final say," she giggled, "but you want your future husband to love the dress almost as much as you do, right?"

She had a point. On the runway earlier that day, Dave's opinion had been the last thing on my mind as I fretted over price tags and imaginary pockets of fat on my arms.

"He always tells me I'm his very own Disney princess," I said. (Um...and Dear Readers, if you ever meet Dave don't mention that to him—he'll tell you he only likes *The Lion King* and *Tarzan,* Disney's more manly selections.)

Bridget grinned. "I have the perfect dress for you."

She turned on the heel of her canvas sneaker and prepared to dive back into the mass of dresses crowded along the far wall of the store.

"Wait!" I said, just as she heaved a row of hangers off to the side. "Is this...this *perfect dress*...under a thousand bucks?"

"Of course!" she said. "Honestly, we don't carry that many gowns over your budget."

I heard my mom's audible sigh of relief at this, but the greedy devil appeared again on my shoulder, hissing, "How can a *cheap* dress look anywhere near as good as the one you had on this morning?" I had to admit to myself that the gown this morning had set the bar pretty high—and it had also set a reference point on price. I could feel myself anchoring on $12,000 as a figure that indicated a level of beauty and quality that less expensive dresses simply lacked. Then I caught Molly's eye as she helpfully held aside a pile of chiffon so Bridget could unearth the dress she had in mind for me.

Molly's gorgeous wedding gown, the raw silk number that made her look like a blond Audrey Hepburn, had been inexpensive—and it had all the bridal bells and whistles, including subtle crystal detailing at the waist, intricate ruching on the bodice and beautiful tailoring that would hold up a few decades from now for her own daughter's wedding.

I brushed aside the selfish devil on my shoulder and stepped into my teeny dressing room. Bridget appeared a moment later, arms full of glittering tulle.

"Most girls don't even want to try on this dress because it's *such* a ball gown," she said, panting from the effort of carrying it. "But for a girl who has Prince Charming waiting for her at the altar, this is The One."

She plopped the dress on the ground, skirt first, and it stayed standing like a mountain of bridey-ness. She unzipped the bodice (I reminded myself it was okay to have a bodice with a zipper instead of buttons or ribbons) and asked me to step in. I closed my eyes and took the plunge—literally. I misjudged how much fabric I had to step over to get into the dress and found myself clawing at the cloth walls of the dressing room, trying to keep my balance without shoving my grundies into Bridget's face. She reached out, grabbed my hand and guided me to the patch of floor buried beneath the layers of ivory netting.

As she zipped me up, I kept my eyes on the floor. I didn't want to see myself until I was standing with my mom and Molly.

Bridget took the back in with industrial-sized clamps. Turns out that at most bridal salons, where you're not expected to be built like a twig, the sample dresses are typically size 10 to 14 to work for any body type. I already felt better about myself. We didn't need any Wiggs-sized crowbars to shove me into *this* gown.

I stepped out of the dressing room, arms held out slightly to accommodate the wide skirt that fell from my hips, and looked at my mom and Molly.

I'm sure you've already guessed what happened.

This time, both of their eyes filled with tears, and I knew they were the good kind.

I stepped up to the trifold mirror and peered at myself.

Would you believe it—this dress was friggin' *better* than the one I'd tried on that morning. It had a more classic line and hit my hips exactly below their natural curve, making me appear as deliciously feminine as any Disney princess. The bodice was covered with silver crystals and embroidery, which, seen from a few steps back, made me shimmer. And my boobs! They looked great! Perky, a little larger than they naturally are, but not like giant melons or anything (I'll take whatever I can get). The skirt was made from layer upon layer of ivory tulle, forming a wide, swishy circle that swirled around my feet as I moved. A chapel-length train floated on the floor behind me, the top layer embroidered with tiny flowers.

It was the dress of my dreams. It was too good to be true.

I gulped. "Okay, how much does it cost?"

"This one is $750."

"Seven hundred fifty...dollars?" I asked, gaping.

I looked at my mom, who was managing to keep herself together. She gave me a small, firm nod. Sha*zam*.

On my wedding day more than a year later, people couldn't stop complimenting me on the dress, I felt glorious about myself and Dave needed CPR the minute he saw me.

My mom, I'm forced to tell you, knew I Do Bridal was a good karma shop as soon as we went to the front of the store to purchase the dress: at the main counter, writing up orders with calm efficiency, was a woman who shared a story about her own daughter's wedding gown. She was a mother, too. And when there's a mom in charge, you can't go wrong.

SUSAN

When Elizabeth found the dress I was thrilled—but not a bit surprised. The moment I saw it, I thought, "Of course."

Why? Because I'd known what the dress would look like since she was five years old. She started drawing pictures of herself as a bride back then, and in every picture she drew, she was wearing this exact dress, practically down to the last detail. There was always a crystal-encrusted bodice surrounded by yards and yards of sparkling tulle, a veil worthy of Maria in *The Sound of Music* and high-heeled dancing shoes.

The most important attribute of the dress, as any little girl will tell you, is that it must bell out gracefully when she spins around. Every time Elizabeth tried on a dress or even a nightgown, she would spin like a dervish. "It swirls," she would say. "It swirls!" If the swirl factor was not present, the garment would go straight back to the rack.

The dress she found had swirl. It had crystals. Beading, tulle, you name it. When she spun around, that sucker swirled clear to Cincinnati. It was, for sure, The One.

The only missing detail was the groom. As a tiny girl, she wasn't picky. In fact, for the longest time, she thought the word was *broom* and decided it was a perfectly good dance partner. The groom might be a large plush toy with button eyes, or our aging Golden Retriever. Sometimes she'd rope in an actual kid. I remember a boy she called Stinkypants in preschool who was willing to stand there like Bambi in the headlights while she twirled around him.

The one thing that never changed was that dress. Twenty years later, the vision came to life in a tiny bridal shop in Seattle, and it was well worth the wait.

It passed the spin test. It *swirled*.

So that's the good news. The bad news is, the mom has to wear *something*. And okay, I'll just say it. Reality bites. You know which reality I mean—the one that glares at you with the unblinking clarity of a three-way mirror in the dressing room.

Most of us don't spend our time in the limelight on a day-to-day basis. So when it smacks you upside the head that you're going to have to look fabulous on your daughter's Big Day, you start to fret. You look in that mirror, illuminated by the least-flattering light ever to beam down on a bulge of cellulite, and fretfulness sets in.

While your size-2 daughter is being outfitted as the Princess Bride, you're feeling like Jabba the Hutt. You start thinking about the thousands of pictures that will be taken, and all of a sudden liposuction doesn't seem like such an unreasonable proposition.

Time for another little consultation with your Common Sense Fairy. Remember that although you're an important part of this day, you're not the most important part. And here's another little tidbit. Do yourself a favor and go look at some photos of people's weddings. The bride is *always* beautiful, isn't she? And the bride's mother looks just magnificent, doesn't she? Even if she's, um, gravitationally challenged and wearing a chiffon monstrosity of a dress, she looks great in the pictures. Here's the key—a photo of someone who is happy and having a great time is always going to look good. Genuine emotion trumps cosmetic surgery every time.

However, you do need a dress. But I'll tell you what you do *not* need. You do not need a chiffon monstrosity. You don't need a drapey muumuu or a bell-sleeved tunic covering up your arms. You don't need something edgy and loud and fashion-forward that calls attention to itself. And you don't—God forbid—want to clash or compete with the groom's mother.

Here's what you do want—you want to look age-appropriate but stylish enough. You want to feel comfortable even six hours into the festivities. You want to *dance.*

I'm a little out of my depth, offering style tips. As a writer, I tend to spend long hours alone in a room, wearing a sweatsuit, fuzzy slippers and headphones. (Sorry about that visual.) I pretty much have the fashion sense of a gas station attendant. And I'd rather watch moss grow on a barn roof than spend a day shopping.

But I'm a quick study and I know how to listen and go to the experts. I'm also a champ at web surfing. So my own personal quest for the dress started there. Once the princess picks her colors, head out on a web safari.

Stick to the palette. This doesn't mean you have to match. You simply don't want to clash. If you're as challenged as I am, check the color wheel. Or better yet, call up your most fashionable friends and ask for their advice.

Steer clear of dedicated bridal stores. No offense to your local "Gowns'R'Us" outlet, but the mother-of-the-bride dresses tend to be, um…dowdylicious, to coin a term.

Nothing screams "I hate my Teutonic butcher's wife arms" more than a claret-colored, bell-sleeved tunic.

Try some off-the-beaten-track shops and designers. Try picking the brain of your daughter's fashionista bridesmaid who works at Nordstrom. Once you narrow down your list to a few options, go ahead and order a few (make sure the store has a fair return policy because you probably won't hit paydirt the first time out). And run them by the princess. Trust me: she has better fashion sense than you do. I ended up wearing a fun but age-appropriate dress in a subtle silk moire print by a newish designer called Leifsdottir. The aforementioned fashionista even found it for me half off at Bloomingdale's, and I felt great in it, even with my brutish arms showing.

Here's a little shopping secret I'm happy to share. You know those shoes? Those incredible, cute, danceable shoes? (Hint: Google "Hey Lady" shoes: www.shopheylady.com.) They do *not* make you look fat. So go ahead and indulge.

Reminder: tell the groom's mom what you're wearing. Only in bad romantic comedies do the moms show up in the same who-wore-it-better gown.

CHEAT SHEET

Too blinded by reams of white satin to read the whole chapter? Here's your cheat sheet:

1. I already said it, and I'll say it again: *a big white dress is a big white dress.* Remember this when you feel a tug in your gut toward that haute couture gown that will put you in the red.

2. Go to the upscale bridal salon—but do your due diligence afterward and see if you can find an equally beautiful dress that isn't overpriced just because your dressing room was the size of a tract mansion.

3. The most beautiful part of your wedding ensemble will be the girl wearing it.

7- 2012